# BOTTLE ROCKET

A So Over the Holidays Novella

---

ERIN MCLELLAN

## *Candy Hearts* (So Over the Holidays #2)

"Candy Hearts *by Erin McLellan is sweet, steamy, totally cute and little bit kinky.*"

—National Public Radio (For February, 3 Romances That Are Short and Candy-Sweet)

"*Erin McLellan delivers again with a sexy and sweet story, filled with humor, heart and hope, for your Valentine's Day reading pleasure.*"

—Layla Reyne, author of the bestselling Fog City Trilogy

"Candy Hearts *is blazing hot Valentine's fun that is jam packed with delightful tropes and sex toys. Exactly the level of heat I needed to melt the winter blues.*"

—Rachel Reid, author of the Game Changers Series

# Blurb

Freshly single Rosie Holiday is on the hunt for passion and excitement. This leads her to Leo Whittaker—a bad boy who waltzed out of town, and her life, thirteen years ago. Leo isn't the type to stick around, but Rosie's not going to let a no-strings opportunity pass her by.

When a business trip sends Leo back to his hometown, the last thing he expects is for his first love to hand him a list of scorching-hot escapades and a deadline. He's happy to help Rosie discover her bossy side in the bedroom. Or in a fireworks stand. Or at a Fourth of July barbecue.

Their chemistry burns bright and fast, but what tore them apart years ago is still between them. They are polar opposites. A reserved kindergarten teacher and an irreverent artist. A nester and a wanderer. It will take a spark of imagination and a lot of love to keep their second-chance romance from flaming out.

*To the Anchoritas: Ashley, Grace, Grace, Kassi, Kathryn, Kaylie, Marina, and Mel*

L eo alternated between eating his sour-cherry snow cone and sipping his lukewarm beer. He liked the taste of the snow cone better, but he wanted the beer. One made him happy, and the other made him reckless. He would choose reckless any day of the week.

He watched as his girlfriend, Rosie, lit a single Black Cat firecracker with a smoldering punk before dancing away from the fuse. The firecracker snapped and flashed. Adrenaline washed over him. He loved blowing shit up. He especially loved watching Rosie—his amazing, dependable, stable Rosie—blow shit up.

She skipped over to him. She'd gotten tan this summer, and her hair was bleached from the sun. She was too good for him.

"Your turn," she said sweetly. Her cheeks were flushed, her eyes big and blue and innocent. He placed his cups in two small holes he'd dug in the sand by the blanket. She handed him the punk and eyed their stash of firecrackers, which was a few feet away from their blanket on the sandy bank of the river.

"I love you, Rosie Posey," he said back. He'd been trying to say it more and more. They were running out of time, and he wanted to make sure she knew it.

She landed in his lap, and he snuffed the punk out in the dirt so he could grab on to her. He found her hipbones under her tiny, low-rise jean shorts.

"I love you too." She nipped his lip, and his heart started to race.

He enjoyed having her above him, and he liked the tiny bite of pain. It made him hot and uncomfortable in equal measure. He didn't really know what it meant.

The sun was setting behind her, and her skin was awash with pink and gold. He tried to memorize the image.

She took a drink of his mostly melted snow cone but ignored his offer of beer. Then she kissed him until his mind was blank of anything but the desire to bury himself in her.

They hadn't had much sex, but they talked about it all the time. What it meant. What felt good. What didn't. They talked about it more than they had it, but he liked that about them.

He loved talking to her. They talked about his California dreams and the songs he was writing and his guitar lessons. They talked about her college admission letter and her parents who she hadn't seen in six years and her little brother who she was so worried about. They talked about the restless itch under Leo's skin. The way he wanted to leave this place and never come back. How he wanted to move and fly and run. That standing still in this dumb fucking town for another day, week, month—it all made him feel as if he were burning alive.

They talked about how she'd helped raise her brother and sister, and how her grandma was run too thin. That Rosie would never leave her family. That she wanted a home that was hers, one that was stable and perfect. She wanted normal—the white picket fence, the mom and dad, husband and wife, the retirement plan, the pretty lawn.

She talked about how she wanted to be loved. He talked about how much he loved her.

But he didn't want to talk about love or sex now. He wanted to feel Rosie's skin under his hands. Right as he reached for her T-shirt, she jumped out of his lap with a smile. She didn't smile often. That was what made the uninhibited ones so precious.

"Smoke bombs," she said. "We need to light them before it gets too dark."

He grabbed the punk out of the sand and relit it with his lighter. "You do it. I wanna watch you."

She preened playfully and made her way over to their stash, grabbing a clear bag of small, colorful balls. He finished his beer, then his snow cone.

She emptied the bag and arranged the smoke bombs in a line. Then she lit every single one until there were billows of rainbow-colored smoke wafting around her.

It was the most beautiful thing Leo had ever seen. He wished he could capture the picture—the powdery smoke caressing her skin, the sunset behind her, the strong lines of her body as she moved—and hold it forever.

His chest started to ache as she shot him another rare smile. He had a plan. It wasn't a well-thought-out plan. Most of his plans weren't. He was going to head to LA and try to be a musician. It was actually the freedom that appealed to him, not the music, but he didn't know what else he was good for. It sure as shit wasn't the crap his parents had planned for him.

Rosie also had a plan. It was a very good one. All her *P*s and *Q*s in place, all the forms filled out to a *T*.

They talked about everything, but they hadn't said the most important words quite yet. They were coming soon though. They were sneaking up on them quickly, each day putting them closer and closer.

He stood and grabbed Rosie around the middle, drowning in her breathless laughs as he picked her up and lowered her to their blanket. Goodbyes were always hard, but this one was going to break his fucking heart.

## Chapter One

Rosie took a deep breath and swung open the wooden door of the community center classroom. This was the Summer of Rosie: Take #6. Still-life painting.

She'd been calling it the "Summer of Rosie" rather than "Mission to Find a Hobby" or "Your Succulents Are Not a Personality," and she was hoping the painting class would go better than the women's choir audition, the mountain biking, the umpiring, the beer brewing, and the improv class.

It wasn't that all of the attempted activities had been a disaster—though the improv class had been *not great*—but she just didn't feel passionate about any of them. She'd woken up in May, the day after the school year ended, and realized there was absolutely nothing in her life she was passionate about.

She loved her job, but it wasn't exciting. She wanted to be excited about something. About lots of somethings.

Still-life painting probably wouldn't be it, but she was determined to try. If this attempt was a failure … well, she was on to the next thing—pottery-making or quilting or flight simulation.

In the past, her summers had been a time for getting lesson plans in order for the coming school year, recovering from burnout, and trying, unsuccessfully, to make her ex-husband happy. Last summer, she'd been neck deep in divorce papers and too sad and exhausted to leave her condo.

Even though it was hard, even though it went against every fiber of her introverted being, she was putting herself out there this summer. She was not going to spend another three months moping on the couch. She was going to do something for herself for once. Not her ex. Not the five-year-olds in her classroom. Not her wonderful siblings.

*Her.*

The room at the community center was empty of people, but easels and chairs were set up in a semi-circle around a raised platform. That platform must have been where the still-life objects would go. The class description had been accompanied by an image of a picnic basket full of watermelon, cherries, apples, and patriotic pinwheels. It wasn't exactly her aesthetic, but she figured her painting wouldn't be good enough to hang anywhere anyway.

A man bustled into the classroom with a large cushion in his hand. "Oh, hello. Are you here for the drawing class?" he asked. He was close to her age and had a very friendly voice.

"Yes."

"Sweet. Grab an easel and make yourself comfortable. We'll start here in a few minutes. I'm the teacher, by the way. Dean Humphries."

"Hi. I'm Rosie."

He nodded, dropped the cushion in the center of the platform, and hurried off. Within a few minutes, more people filed into the room. Most seemed to know each other, which sent anxiety spiraling through her. She hated being the odd one out, which made *joining* existing groups or teams very difficult.

Dean came back in and greeted the class. He was handsome. Soulful eyes, sharp nose, a thin cleft lip scar, golden stubble. It wouldn't be a hardship to listen and watch him for the next hour.

When she had told her younger sister, Sasha, about the Summer of Rosie, Sasha had said that one of her new hobbies should be getting laid. Rosie had laughed at the time but hadn't taken it seriously. Now, when she spotted attractive men, that joke felt like a pebble in her shoe— small but distracting. A sex life—a *passionate* sex life—that would be worth celebrating.

Maybe great sex could be the climax of the Summer of Rosie. *Ha.* Too bad she would never have the nerve to go out and get some.

Dean explained that the art utensils they would need were at the back of the class and students could take their pick. Then he said, "Before I get our model, I'd like to remind everyone to treat him with the utmost respect. I'm going to pass around the class etiquette contract. Please read it, sign it, and pass it back."

Rosie sat up straight. A sudden dread filled her chest. She grabbed her phone out of her pocket to check if she was in the wrong room.

She reread the description on the events page for the community center, but nothing there seemed awry. Dean was passing out copies of the contract and pens.

Rosie leaned over to her neighbor, showed her the phone, and said, "Is this the still-life painting class?"

The woman beside her squinted at the phone before saying, "No. That's tomorrow and is a beginner class. See, June thirtieth in the description? Today is June twenty-ninth. This class is Intermediate Figure Drawing. We draw a different nude model every week."

"Oh shit."

This was what happened when her week wasn't dictated by a kindergarten classroom. She couldn't keep her Mondays straight from her Tuesdays or Wednesdays or Thursdays.

Now she had a dilemma. She could stick this out, try to draw a nude person, and move on to the Summer of Rosie: Take #7. Or she could leave immediately. The class was free, and the whole purpose of her little experiments this summer was to experience new things. Find passion in life. Fill the hole where her marriage used to be. On the other hand, this class would be way out of her depth, and, because she was an amateur artist, she suspected it would be insensitive to stay.

Before she could make her move, she was handed a

contract to sign, and Dean, who had stepped out, reentered the classroom with a dark-headed man in tow. She couldn't see the other guy clearly through Dean, but the hem of a navy silk robe fluttered around his shins.

Dean spoke quietly to the model for a few seconds before stepping out of the way to collect the contracts. Without hesitation, the model took off his robe. Rosie felt rude looking at the man straight on. She also felt rude leaving too abruptly. What if he thought she was offended by his nakedness?

She would have to sneak out. Maybe she could claim to need a bathroom break and not come back.

In her peripheral vision, she caught a smattering of black, delicate tattoos across the model's pale chest, arms, and hands. He had nice hands. He sat down on the cushion and leaned back, his whole body on display. She blushed, reacting to the weird situation and her own embarrassment. Her gaze snapped up to his face because that seemed the safest place to look.

It was not.

Her vision wavered, the room going blurry.

It was like her mind was separate from her body, because she absolutely did not mean to stand up and send her chair scraping back on the tile floor. The racket was overwhelming, but it took an extended beat for the noise to fully reach her.

Every muscle in her body wound tight. She was hot. It was hot, right? Too hot.

She glanced around. Everyone was staring at her. *Everyone.* Including the nude man in the middle of the room, who also happened to be … her first? What did you call the adult version of the teenager you lost your heart to over a decade ago?

*A walking naked nightmare, that's what.*

Fuck, she'd never expected to see him again. Fuck.

Dean rushed over. "Are you okay?"

She nodded too vehemently. "Yeah, sorry. I'm sorry. I'm in the wrong class. I thought I'd be painting a fruit basket."

Dean laughed softly. "No worries. This must be a shock. That class is tomorrow."

"Okay." She couldn't remember where she'd put her purse. Had she brought a purse?

"You're welcome to stay if you're comfortable. I can talk you through beginner techniques."

Rosie chanced a peek at the middle of the room. Leo Whittaker—her first boyfriend and now community center nude model—seemed just as stricken.

"No, thank you. I appreciate it, but I know the model. Hi." She waved at Leo. He didn't move. "So, yep, this has officially hit my limit on the awkwardness scale."

Dean turned to Leo in surprise. The whole class was watching the exchange like it was a tetherball match. Leo slowly shrugged back into the silk robe, covering himself up.

"Rosie?" Leo's voice was rougher than she remembered. Hardened and smoky. It sent a shiver down her spine. He stood up. His presence was overwhelming. He wasn't a tall man, but he had charisma. Even in a silk robe and bare feet, he was imposing.

She felt naked, which was absurd. She wasn't the one who had exposed her body to a room full of artists, but she felt as if everyone could see all the messed up bits inside her.

"Yeah. Hi. Okay. I'm going to go."

Every attempt at finding a hobby, connection, and passion had been a dud, but none of them had been inherently embarrassing. Shit like this didn't happen to her. She was controlled and reserved and honestly a bit boring. Her siblings were going to have a field day if they found out about this.

She spun on her heels and took off.

"Rosie, wait. Hold—" Leo's voice cut off as the door closed behind her.

Leo Whittaker had run off to California thirteen years ago, leaving her behind. Damn. What was he doing back in town?

Her mind swirled as she strode down the hallway. At eighteen, Leo had been a bad boy. He'd shot potato cannons on the golf course. He'd stolen smokes from his mom. He'd hot-boxed with his friends. He'd done everything in his power to rebel against the high-class expectations of his very wealthy family, including running around with a girl from the wrong side of the tracks. But he hadn't looked like a bad boy back then.

He *looked* like a bad boy now.

"Rosie Holiday!"

Leo's voice pulled her up short, as did his use of her maiden name. She'd legally changed her name back after her divorce, but it sometimes surprised her when she

11

heard it. She spun to face him. He was standing there in bare feet, the robe wrapped tightly around him. A hysterical laugh bubbled up inside her. He grinned and jogged to catch up with her.

As soon as he was within a few feet, she said, "Oh my God, I'm so sorry if I embarrassed you. I was not prepared for that."

"I wasn't prepared for you either."

"What are you doing here?" she asked, a thick, unnamed emotion in her voice.

"I'm friends with Dean and owed him a favor."

"Wow. Big favor."

"Glad you noticed."

She laughed again and touched her forehead. Her hands were shaking. "There is not a single friend for whom I'd drop trou in a room full of strangers."

"Nakedness doesn't bother me." He gifted her his trademark ornery smile.

Youthful summertime memories rushed up on her. Cool river water against her bare skin. The scent of sunscreen and condoms. Sour-cherry-flavored kisses. The snap of firecrackers against hot sand.

Rosie rolled her eyes. She was a sucker for that smile. Made her feel nostalgic. "Oh, shut up. What brings you home?"

"This hasn't been home in a long time," he said.

"I'm aware."

"I'm here for six days for work."

Days. She and Leo Whittaker in the same place for

*days*. Stupid possibilities bombarded her. The main one, to her surprise, was sex.

She could have sex with Leo Whittaker. Summer of Rosie: Take #69. It would be awesome.

Too bad she was a total coward. Figure drawing was not going to be her thing. Neither was hooking up with old flames.

Probably.

Unless he wanted to.

"Rosie?" His gaze was eating her up, running a fast circuit from her face to her shoulders and throat. Maybe that was heat in his eyes? Or maybe it was discomfort?

She was so bad at this.

"Yeah?"

"Are you still married?"

She blinked a few times in surprise and touched her naked ring finger with her thumb. How did he know she'd been married? They hadn't spoken since their breakup, which meant he'd checked up on her at some point in the last decade.

"No. Divorced." In the past, that word had tasted like ash in her mouth, but now it was a relief.

"I'm sorry," he said.

She waved the apology away. "It was for the best. Trust me."

He bit his lip. "Remember when I left notes in your work locker for two weeks before you gave me a second glance?"

"Yeah, you were a big weirdo."

He laughed. He had a tattoo that snaked up the side

of his throat. His hair was as dark as when they'd been teenagers, but he no longer had the Sunday-school cut his mother had insisted on. He had an undercut with wild wavy locks that grazed his chin. A gold ring graced his full bottom lip and thick stubble highlighted his sharp jaw. He looked different, but he had the same moss-green eyes. The same long lashes. The same crooked smile and deep dimples. Seeing him like this, so unexpected, yet so welcome, sent a tremor of longing through her.

"You were a relentless pest," Rosie said.

"I remember you liking it."

"Teenagers can be stupid."

He laughed again, and she let out a shaky breath. She wasn't sure what it meant, Leo showing up in her life at this moment. Her siblings, both of whom were annoyingly coupled up, would say it was a sign. She didn't believe in signs anymore. Or fate. Or flighty bad boys who craved freedom. She was the arbiter of her own happiness, her own security now. Leo was temptation and danger personified, but damn, it was good to see him.

His humor faded, and he stared at her with an intensity that was all new. "I really want to hug you, but I know that might be weird, considering the circumstances."

She practically launched herself at him, giving him a quick, fierce hug.

"Fuck, Rosie." He hugged her back hard, his cheek grazing hers and the silk of his robe slipping over her skin.

She'd loved him so much when they'd been eighteen, but

they'd been just that—*eighteen*. Thankfully, they'd been smart enough to realize their lives were heading in opposite directions, and he'd cut ties with her rather than let their individual needs tear them apart. All her experiences with romantic love, with the exception of Leo, had torn her apart.

"I have to get back in there," he said, glancing behind him to the room of waiting artists.

"It was nice to see you." She grimaced. The words sounded empty, but they weren't.

"This class is over in an hour."

"Okay."

"Can I see you after?"

Her pulse jumped. "Okay." She needed to learn a different word, but damn.

He started walking backwards, a grin on his face. "Meet you out front, by the garden area?"

She eyed him. "You're still trouble, Leo Whittaker. I won't forget."

"But you'll be there?"

"I'll be there."

Rosie found her way to the community garden in a daze. She didn't know there was a community garden. The fact that Leo did was fucking her up.

She found a wooden bench in the shade. A morning breeze wafted through her hair. She had an hour to kill, which was just enough time to thoroughly freak the fuck out.

Was this a date? Dating had not been on the agenda this summer. It was an obstacle course out there, and she was not equipped. Plus, Leo was only in town for a few days. She didn't even know where he lived.

She took a deep breath. She needed to slow her roll.

This would be two old friends catching up. No biggie.

Too bad he was so hot.

Maybe this could be a fling. *A summer fling.*

A booty call! Was ten in the morning the time booty calls happened when you were in your thirties?

If she'd been *planning* for a booty call, she would have worn her new bra. She would have brought gum.

Recklessness pushed against Rosie's chest. She was never reckless. She was calculated. Dependable. Reserved. She'd always had to be. Her parents had bailed when she was young, and her grandmother had worked multiple jobs to make ends meet. It was why she craved security so much as an adult.

Her siblings said she had oldest-child syndrome, and that might have been true, but mostly, she hated to feel out of control.

Today, though, that recklessness tasted sweet on her tongue. This was her chance to truly live her life. To open herself up to new experiences and find herself. If that led to fucking an old boyfriend after accidentally crashing a figure-drawing class where he was the nude model, all the better. She grabbed her phone and pulled up her text thread with Sasha. She started debating with herself in her head, thinking about logistics and travel time.

Maybe she had time to run home. She checked her watch. It would be close, especially with the construction in the area, and she was worried that if she weren't there when Leo finished, he would think she'd ghosted. She couldn't exactly be-bop back into that room to tell him she'd be right back.

Rosie took a deep breath and thumbed out a message. Sasha had gotten back from her honeymoon four days ago and had one more day before she started working again.

*Hey. What are you doing?*

Sasha: *Watching my slacker finish the homework he missed due to wedded bliss.*

Rosie adored Sasha's new husband, and she knew for a fact he was not a slacker.

Rosie: *Can you do me a favor? I'm at the community center. Will you swing by my place and grab a bra for me?*

Sasha: *Did yours break? Any preference on which, because I will choose your sluttiest if you don't give me instructions.*

Rosie bit back a smile. Sasha worked for a sex toy and lingerie company called Lady Robin's Intimate Implements. Rosie could rely on her to be raunchy. Luckily, her sluttiest bra was exactly what Rosie wanted.

Rosie: *Baby blue lace on top of my dresser. Also, do you have mints?*

Sasha: *ROSIE!*

Sasha: *Do you have a date? An obscenely early morning date?*

Sasha: *OMG*

Rosie smiled. When Sasha was excited, she texted in hurried spurts. Rosie had no idea if it was a date, but she hadn't been this thrilled over the possibility of a date, or what a date could lead to, in years. Rosie didn't have time to respond before Sasha hit her with another flurry of messages.

Sasha: *I'll be there in thirty.*

Sasha: *Lube!*

Sasha: *I have samples of our new lube.*

Sasha: *I'm bringing some.*

Sasha: *Just in case. It's good lube.*

Sasha: *TRUST. ME.*

Sasha: *Summer of Rosie Needing Good Lube*

Rosie laughed helplessly. She loved her sister, but seeing the words made the possibility of her "needing good lube" seem ridiculous. She didn't want to get her hopes up.

Rosie: *Not a date.*

Rosie: *But bring the lube.*

## Chapter Two

Leo found Rosie easily enough. She was sitting on a bench under a large shade tree, the sun spackling her through the leaves. Nostalgia hooked him and pulled at his chest. It felt like he'd traveled back in time.

He'd been so surprised to see her earlier that he hadn't been able to look his fill. But no doubt—Rosie Holiday was still an absolute smoke show. The prim-and-proper thing had always done it for him. Hell, Rosie was probably the inspiration for that origin story. Every buttoned-up crush since had been because of her.

Leo grinned and sat beside her. Rosie narrowed her eyes, and happiness burst inside him. He loved that challenge in her expression. Always had.

"Hey, Rosie Posey."

"God, Leo. Do not call me that."

He laughed. "You sound exactly the same."

"Oh yeah? How's that?"

"Like a stern teacher who's real good at putting me in

my place." He loved a nice sharp voice, and Rosie's cut through him perfectly.

"I am a teacher."

He paused. "I'm so glad, Rosie. I know that was your plan."

They'd broken up because he'd wanted to be the wayfaring rebel. He had a drive inside him that compelled him to run away. After a childhood full of uncertainty and struggle, she'd needed a soft spot to land, a stable home, a steady career. He'd scurried off to LA, and she'd gone to college to become a teacher. He was glad their separate paths had worked out, but it bitter-sweet at the same time.

A comfortable silence stretched between them. He took the opportunity to study her, to find and delight in the ways she'd changed. The ways she hadn't.

She was wearing a cornflower-blue tank top. It made her guarded, pale blue eyes pop and drew his attention to her throat. Her hair was cut into a chin-length bob that enhanced her delicate collarbones and freckle-speckled shoulders. He itched to paint that slope of neck and shoulder. To turn it into something he could capture and keep. Something hot. Something totally different than the drawings Dean's students had churned out.

His art was the reason he was back in his hometown for more than a weekend stopover. He loved being an artist. He got a lot of joy out of creating for other people and traveling the country from one adult novelty conven-tion to the next. He still had that impulse to put peddle to the metal and chase the newest muse, but that hadn't been as fulfilling lately. It felt important that he'd run into Rosie. As if seeing her was exactly where and what he was meant to be doing. He was enough of a hippie-dippy free spirit to follow his gut, and his gut was guiding him right to her.

His and Rosie's relationship had been a secret when they'd been teenagers. Back then, he'd never met her siblings. Yet, in a few days, he'd be selling his erotic art at a Lady Robin's Independence Day popup shop, which had been organized by Rosie's sister, Sasha. Lady Robin's was his newest partnership. He ran in the same social and professional circles as Robin Erco, the owner of Lady Robin's. It was all very convoluted and interconnected, but he'd fully expected to make it through this hometown visit without seeing Rosie Holiday.

A ladybug landed on Rosie's shoulder, stark against her skin. She looked like a Disney character—a princess with beautiful creatures flocking to her. He imagined drawing her as Snow White at the well, her peaches-and-cream complexion, her not-so-innocent expression. That type of stylized character art was his bread and butter.

She frowned and brushed the bug off her arm, poised, practical, and unbothered. He would have been excited to find a ladybug on his arm. She'd shooed it off with no fanfare.

All the reasons he'd loved her at eighteen smacked him in the fucking face.

"Whitt!" Dean called out Leo's nickname in his deep, melodic voice. Both he and Rosie jumped.

Leo waved at his friend, and Dean approached them,

a smile on his handsome face. In the past, when Leo passed through town to visit his parents, he usually spent a night with Dean. Their relationship was easy and supportive. Dean knew him, understood him, and Leo suspected today's interruption had made him incredibly curious.

"Hi y'all. Sorry about the surprise today, Rosie," Dean said.

"It's fine. I'm sorry for causing a scene. I'm normally a little more chill."

Dean's smile was too excited for Leo's liking.

"How do you two know each other?" Dean asked.

She paused for an awkward second before saying, "I worked for Leo's parents at Froth and Forage when we were both in high school."

Leo bit the inside of his lip, fiddling with the edge of his piercing with his tongue. He hated that that was how she'd described their relationship, but what had he expected her to say?

*We lost our virginity to each other over a decade ago.*

*I told him I loved him when we were teenagers.*

*He was a fuck up, and I had my shit together.*

"Oh yeah," Dean said. "I love Froth and Forage. We torment his parents by drinking at the bar there when he's in town."

Rosie seemed surprised by that.

Yes, Leo was still tormenting his parents, but in incredibly harmless ways, like laughing too loudly at their restaurant with one of his best friends and buying his mother silver spoon knick-knacks from weird places, which she promptly threw in a plastic bin in his old room.

"What about you guys? How do you know each other?" she asked, then glanced at Leo. "I assumed you didn't come home that often."

There was that word again. *Home*. He'd been searching for a place that felt like home for thirteen years. This sure as shit wasn't it.

Dean gestured to Leo, indicating he should take the lead on this, which Leo appreciated. He didn't want to blurt out that they'd met at a fuck party six years ago.

"We met through mutual friends in the erotic art world."

Rosie didn't react to that. She was a pro at schooling her expressions. Or she used to be. He didn't really know her anymore.

His heart was fighting him on that point. He knew that at eighteen the best thing he could do for her was leave. He knew that she would move the moon for her siblings. He knew that when she was nervous, she fiddled with the hair behind her ears. He knew that kissing this one particular spot between her shoulder blades would make her wet. He knew that she was stingy with her real smiles, which made each one a precious fucking gift.

He'd been enamored by her at eighteen. Through the years, he'd imagined seeing her again, holding her again, making her smile again. He'd imagined coming back to her as an adult with the full knowledge of his desires and needs and predilections, and in those dreams, she was into it. He inwardly laughed at himself. *If only.*

"I'm sorry," she said. "You're an erotic artist, Leo? What happened to being a musician?"

Dean's mouth dropped open. "I'm sorry," he echoed her. "You wanted to be a musician, Leo?"

A beat of silence passed between them before laughter overtook it. The giggles started with Rosie and quickly spread to him and Dean. It was surreal, these different time periods of his life crashing into each other.

"I am an artist," Leo said.

"A good one," Dean chimed in.

Leo ignored the praise. "And I ran away at eighteen to busk on street corners, which did nothing except horrify my parents—a plus—and teach me how to handle hecklers. I sucked."

"You know what this means, don't you?" Dean asked. Leo rolled his eyes. He recognized where this was leading. "You owe me a performance. You've been hiding your light under a bushel, and I, for one, will not stand for it. Did you write your own music? Oh, who am I kidding? Of course you did."

"Lots of metaphors," Rosie said matter-of-factly.

"What?" Dean said, a maniacal light in his eyes. He was enjoying this too much.

"His songs were all metaphors. My favorite was this one about clouds on the tip of a mountaintop. It was also somehow about sex. Maybe breasts? Do you remember it, Leo?"

Leo shook his head and laughed helplessly.

"Oh my God, can we be best friends?" Dean said to her.

"Sure." She shrugged, cool and unbothered, but in an overtly playful way as if best friendship was just her due.

He saw that Dean was taken by her, that he was sizing her up and trying to figure out exactly how she fit in Leo's past, and if she could fit into his present.

"I have pictures of him too," she said. "From back then. He had this church-boy haircut. He looked so innocent, but he was *so bad*." She shot Leo one of her rare smiles. "I liked it."

"Goddamn, I've missed you," Leo said. The words escaped before he could swallow them back, but fuck.

"And on that note, I'm gonna go," Dean said. "Text me later, Whitt."

Dean left them, and awkwardness followed.

"He calls you Whitt," she said quietly.

"Most people do. I'm known by my last name professionally."

She scrunched her nose up in the cutest way. "I have a lot of questions about that, but they can wait. Should I call you Whitt?"

"No. I like that you call me Leo. It feels …"

"Nostalgic?"

"Yeah. But in a good way."

"Okay, then. Leo it is."

"Speaking of nostalgia, you know what I would kill for?" he asked.

"What?"

"A snow cone."

A trace of confusion zipped through her eyes. Did she expect something different? Maybe she thought he'd suggest skinny-dipping or getting trashed by the river or drag racing, but he wasn't that lost kid any longer. Snow cones were more his speed at ten in the morning. Though skinny-dipping—he could have gone for that. Maybe after lunch.

"Sounds good," she said.

They walked to the parking lot, and he stopped by his motorcycle—a new Triumph Bonneville Speed Twin.

She took a step back. "You expect me to get on that thing?"

He actually didn't. He didn't have protective gear for her legs, and she was in shorts, but he took a second to tease her. "Come on, Rosie. Where's the wild child I remember? I have an extra helmet."

Her tinkling laugh drifted over him, sending a cascade of prickles down his spine. She leaned closer and whispered, "I think not. I do not like being a passive passenger. Plus, you were the wild child, Leo." Her voice was teasing but also authoritative in a way that slipped under his skin. The kinky part of him perked up as if it had been prodded awake.

"You want the keys? I don't mind giving up control. Handing over the reins," he whispered back. He was not talking about his bike anymore, sending out some insinuation to see if she'd bite.

Rosie frowned, a sweet, confused expression on her face. "I don't have my motorcycle license. Why don't we meet there?"

He laughed. Talk about a swing and a miss.

THE SNOW CONE stand was in the lot of a local park. When Leo had last been in this area, there was rusty playground equipment and not much else, but now it was a gorgeous space with a large walking-trail system. There were a few picnic tables close by under a huge cottonwood. The differences thirteen years could make.

They made it to the front of the line, and Leo was pummeled by a memory.

"Rosie," he said, his voice low and urgent.

"Yes?"

"Can I order for you?"

"Only if I get to return the favor."

"You're on."

He stepped up to the open window of the stand. The worker popped her gum and gave them a bored hello.

"A medium sour-cherry snow cone, please," he said.

Rosie nudged his shoulder with her own, which he took as a win.

Sour-cherry snow cones had been their thing. They'd eaten them constantly that last summer they'd spent together. They'd been sharing a sour-cherry snow cone the first time they'd fooled around. He'd gone down on her that night and discovered the miracle of oral sex. Thinking about it sent a sense memory to his taste buds. Sour cherry and Rosie's distinctly beachy flavor on the back of his tongue. He'd never forget that moment. He enjoyed fuck clubs and sex parties and drew erotic art of his friends and had slept with a hugely diverse array of people in his life, but those first experiences with Rosie were special in a way very few had been since.

He wondered if she tasted the same.

He needed to get control before he threw himself at her feet. He didn't have a love life currently. He had a sex life. It wasn't fair to start a fling with Rosie if she didn't understand the reasons for that.

He wondered what sour-cherry memory was in the back of her mind. The last time they'd seen each other, the night before he'd driven to California, she'd finished his snow cone and kissed him until their mouths were sore. He'd never said the word goodbye. He'd just left with the taste of her on his lips.

Rosie stepped up to the window next and ordered him a medium silver-fox snow cone. He quirked his eyebrow. Her order for him seemed random. She reached up and touched the edge of his jaw with her thumb, and his heart shot to his throat.

"Grey."

He laughed. "Can I tell you a secret?"

"Always."

"I'm vain. I'd been coloring that patch on my beard with one of those at-home kits from Walgreens, but I decided to start shaving instead to save money. You're seeing a few days of stubble so the gray is coming through."

Her eyes flashed with delight. "One, the stubble is a good look on you. Two, so is that little spot of silver. You

28

should not waste money to hide your hotness. That's illogical."

"Hotness, huh?"

"You own a mirror, Leo Whittaker."

Tension arced between them until the snow-cone girl said, "Dudes," to get their attention.

Leo grabbed his silver fox and passed the sour cherry over to Rosie. He followed her to a picnic table. She sat up on the tabletop, rather than on one of the benches, her legs dangling off the end. He moved to stand between her legs without thought. It was automatic. They'd been in that position so many times in the six months they'd snuck around as teenagers—her sitting and him standing in the vee of her thighs. But now, they both froze as his actions caught up with them.

"I'm sorry," he said, his voice ragged. He started to take a step back from her, but she stopped him with a hand on his shoulder. Fire rushed through him, lighting him up where her palm held him in place.

"I missed you too. I didn't say that earlier, and I should have," she said. "You're not on social media. I tried to find you while I was waiting for the figure-drawing class to finish."

He took a bite of his snow cone, savoring the vanilla-almond sweetness of the silver-fox syrup. "I used to have personal profiles on every social media platforms, but now I only have them under my professional name. I checked your Facebook probably every other day for years after we broke up," he admitted.

"Really? I figured you'd left and never looked back."

She tucked her hair behind her ear, and his fingers itched to trace the silky strands.

He wasn't the most honest with people. He kept parts of himself stowed away, only releasing them when his paintbrush touched a canvas or his pencil a sketchpad, but he found he didn't have a filter with her. He wanted to be an open book. He wanted her to touch all his pages.

"You were a cornerstone for me. A reminder that someone cared about me, even though we weren't together. I loved to see what you were up to in college." Her profile picture for years had been a photo of her wearing a collegiate sweatshirt over a collared shirt with a small, secret smile on her face. He had often stared at it while trashed off his gourd, wishing for simpler times. Then later, he'd sketched it from memory once her profile picture changed to one from her wedding.

"You should have reached out," she said.

He lightly drew a circle around her kneecap. They should stop touching each other, at least until they had a frank conversation about what it meant. He pulled his hand away. She grabbed it and placed it back on her knee, a dash of defiance in the set of her jaw.

He loved that she was demanding his touch. It sent a strange pang through his stomach.

"I was a disaster," he said. "Fucking around with lots of people, doing drugs, partying, ignoring my parents, couch surfing. I wasn't reliable, and you're so reliable. It wouldn't have been right to pull you into my bullshit. If I had, I would have sucked all that steadfastness out of you until we were both empty. I would have used you up, and that's not something I could fathom. I loved you too much."

He wasn't ashamed of his past or his present. He'd needed to make mistakes back then, but there had been so many times he'd almost phoned her, almost come home and asked her to take him back. But he hadn't, and now there was the distance of thirteen years between them.

"I'm less of a disaster now," he said, when she didn't respond. "I've scaled down to a general low-key mess."

She ate her snow cone and studied him. In between bites, her fingers toyed with the shoulder seam of his shirt.

"What are you thinking about, Rosie?"

Her eyebrows hitched down. "Your parents' constraints stifled you. I'm not surprised you pushed some boundaries once you had the freedom to do so." Her hand trailed to the side of his neck, her thumb on his Adam's apple. "I also appreciate that you didn't use me as an emotional crutch. My ex-husband did that to me. Used my love for him to make himself feel better, especially when he was fucking up."

Leo frowned, a shaky, unsteady anger washing through him. "Sounds like he sucked."

A laugh slipped from her. "Understatement."

"Love shouldn't be used as a weapon."

"No." She set her Styrofoam cup down beside her and leaned back on her hands. The loss of her palm on him felt like the end of the world. She tipped her head back, obviously enjoying the summer heat on her skin. "Where are you staying while you're here?"

He drew the hollow of her throat in his mind. Imagined how to replicate the shine of her skin in the bright light, the bottomless blue in her eyes.

"A KOA campground. I live in an Airstream trailer."

"You're kidding."

"I'm not."

She laughed. "That is so perfect for you."

"Yeah, I love it."

"So I'm guessing you don't do music anymore?"

Warmth rushed up his cheeks. "That didn't last long. You should have told me not to run away to LA to be a musician. I was *not good*, and you were the most practical person I knew."

"I thought you were good. You wrote songs about me. Even practical people enjoy flattery."

"Damn. How misguided we both were."

There was a softness around her mouth that made Leo want to kiss her.

"Tell me about the art," she said.

He studied her, trying to detect any judgment in her eyes. A lot of people didn't understand it, but Rosie's expression was steady as ever.

"I have a few coffee table books and make a calendar every year. I do commissions and sell at adult novelty and kink conventions. Sometimes, I get hired to make marketing and product art. Essentially, I have a million side hustles, but they all center around erotic drawings or paintings of people."

"My sister works in the adult novelty world. She sells sex toys."

He nodded. "I know. I'm creating steampunk marketing images for Lady Robin's, and selling my books at their Fourth of July pop-up shop. I'm friends with Robin, and I've emailed with your sister a bit."

Her mouth dropped open, and he worried that he'd screwed up. Then she laughed. "That's crazy. Small world."

She downed the rest of her snow cone. It colored her lips a vivid red. As she set her cup aside, her bra strap slipped down her arm. It was baby blue and shiny. He fixed it for her, and her breath caught, a blush blazing over her cheeks.

"I'd love to—"

"Can I be—"

"You first," Leo said.

She bit her lip and frowned. He wished he could soothe that bitten lip with his tongue, but that was his horniness talking.

"I was going to ask if I could be frank with you," she said. Her words were formal, but there was an underlying tension in her voice.

"Of course."

"I'd love to see your RV … like, now."

Leo leaned back to see her more clearly. A sly smile briefly appeared on her face.

"Gotta shoot my shot, am I right?" she said.

Maybe her horniness was talking too. There was definitely a conversation to be had.

## Chapter Three

Rosie had no idea what she was doing. Well, that wasn't totally true. Currently, she was following Leo to the KOA at the outskirts of the city. To see his RV. That he lived in. Like one of those people on *Tiny House Hunters*. An RV that was hopefully full of his art.

Thoughts pinged around in her head. Not full thoughts, but comic book bubbles of desire: *kiss me, stubble on my thighs, stern teacher, sour cherry, kiss me.*

She was pretty sure she was going to kiss Leo Whittaker. She *wanted* to kiss him. She wanted to shove his head between her legs and order him to lick her to orgasm, if she were honest, but she wasn't quite that bold.

Maybe she should be. Maybe the Summer of Rosie needed a big dose of oral sex. That could be her newest hobby—discovering her clitoris again.

She hadn't felt this horny in … years? Her sex life with Landon had not been great during the final gasps of their marriage. Every fuck had been wrapped up in an argument, which, granted, had sometimes been hot. Those moments of anger and hurt and sex had ripped her apart afterward, made her feel vulnerable, but not in a healthy way. Not in the way sex should.

So yeah, coping with that by following her long lost sweetheart to the woods to bang sounded super smart and healthy.

Leo's sleek, silver Airstream was parked behind a big pickup, and she watched as he wheeled his motorcycle to the back of the campsite.

He smiled as she met him at the door of the trailer. He'd grown an inch or so since they were eighteen. He used to be shorter than her, but now they were the same height. His body was wiry and powerful, and he looked so comfortable in his own skin. The summer sun gilded his dark eyelashes and enhanced the green of his eyes. He was fucking yummy, basically.

He sat on the Airstream's step and held her hips between his hands.

"Quick chat, okay?" he asked.

She nodded.

Was he pumping the breaks? That was fine. She was well acquainted with rejection, but it might take a bottle of wine and a vibrator to get over it tonight.

"I'm assuming something hot is gonna happen when we get in there. I have a good bill of health, and I get tested often."

Oh. She hadn't even thought about that, which was a true testament to how long she'd been out of the dating game.

"I was tested about a year ago after … I mean … Everything was fine, and I haven't been with anyone since."

Leo's head was tipped back to study her. He was certainly reading all kinds of truths in her hesitation. It wasn't the end of the world to say, "Hey, I haven't had sex since my ex-husband. He cheated on me a lot," but she preferred that Leo just make an inference, and they could move along.

"I need to make sure we're on the same page," Leo said. A hint of vulnerability flashed through his eyes, and he let her see it. He didn't hide it. She wanted that openness. Wanted to be able to have that in a partner and show it herself. "I don't live here," Leo continued. "I don't want you to expect—"

"Stop."

His fingers tightened on her hips.

She swallowed hard and made a face. "I don't expect you to be my boyfriend, Leo."

Silence hit her. Then Leo's shaky breath. "You're too good for me, Rosie Holiday."

She glanced at him sharply. "I like when you call me that. My maiden name."

"Then I'll keep doing it. I'm a people pleaser."

"And I want you to please me."

His expression went a bit feral. "The things I'm into during sex are not exactly run of the mill."

She smiled. If he was talking about butt stuff, she had news for him—he was not that special. "How so?"

"I like to give up control. Maybe be slapped around a

36

little. Ordered around a lot. Nothing too wild, but some people balk. I'm into group sex too, but that's neither here nor there."

She hadn't been expecting that. Sweat bloomed along her spine. She was suddenly aware she was above him and he was sitting at her feet. She liked it.

And group sex? It would be a big fat lie to claim she'd never thought about it. It would be impossible to not think about it if you were in any way acquainted with Sasha's boss, Robin Erco, who was notorious for throwing orgies.

Rosie started to open her mouth to speak, but closed it quickly. She had so many thoughts clanging around inside her head.

"Be honest, Rosie," Leo said.

"What if I don't know how to be what you want me to be?" She wanted to try.

"Oh, no. That's not what—I want you to be yourself. I want to make you happy. But I also might ask you to step on me. Hypothetically." She had to bite her lip against a smile. He smiled back, his eyes positively eye-fucking her. "I can be in charge. I can adapt. I'm pretty flexible, for all intents of the word. I was just telling you what I enjoy the most, and I also think you could take control, if you wanted to."

Summer of Rosie: femdom edition.

"I'm trying new things this summer," she blurted. "I'm calling it the Summer of Rosie." Leo's eyes flared with confusion, so she kept talking before she chickened out. "It's an attempt at saying 'no thanks' less and instead chasing 'the yes.' That's what this podcast I listen to says."

"I don't understand."

She sighed. "Divorce is hard, Leo. It fucked me up, made me feel like a blank slate. I want a hobby. I want to be passionate about something. Damn, anything! I want to put you in your place and have group sex and wear out my vibrator. I'm so tired of being ..."

"Being what?"

"Boring."

He frowned, looking fierce and angry, and she wanted to wipe that scowl off his face with her tits.

"Try again. You are not boring."

"Scared. I'm tired of being scared. I want to experience life, rather than letting it pass me by."

"I leave on the fifth of July."

She had to recalibrate at the change in subject. "Okay."

"That means we have six days until I leave."

"Yes."

"I bet you and I could have lots of experiences in that time. Give me six days, no strings."

"Are you saying you want to help me with the Summer of Rosie?" she asked.

"Yes. I do." He slid his hands up under her top to rest lightly on her sides.

"That can be arranged."

"Come inside with me, Rosie." His voice dropped to a deep, gravelly growl. It hit her in the gut ... if her gut was about a foot lower and located in her pussy.

"Lead on."

Leo held her hand as they entered the Airstream. He flipped a light on. The inside was unexpected. She'd pictured flowered polyester booths and cheap wood paneling and yellow light. Or maybe lots of black leather and dark wood and stainless steel. Instead, the space was light and airy, minimalistic, and full of pastels and fresh flowers. The rounded ceiling was covered in pale wood. A big bed took up one end of the trailer and a lounge area with cushy bench seats dominated the other. There was a tiny galley kitchen and a bathroom in between.

"Wow." She turned in a circle, trying to take everything in at once. The whole trailer was designed with usability and space saving in mind. It was great but also highlighted everything that had ever pulled her and Leo apart. He could put his bike in the back of this baby and follow his heart to the next KOA campground. Her heart needed more consistency than that. She was a nester.

But she still wanted to fuck Leo until he couldn't walk.

"I don't show my place to many people."

"Why not?"

"It's kind of personal in here. My sanctuary, I guess you could say. My constant. And also my studio. I don't want other people's energy to screw it up for me."

That sounded like woo-woo artist talk, but she understood. She'd had to move out of her and Landon's home, even though she could have stayed after he'd left, because bad memories followed her around.

"Is my energy going to mess it up?" she asked.

"No. Your energy is turning me on. I trust you."

If those weren't the sexiest words in the universe … "I trust you too." A tiny shelf stacked with coffee table books caught her eye. She grabbed the book on top and almost dropped it as a parade of realizations walloped her at once. "My sister owns this book."

The cover was a vibrant and very detailed illustration of a topless pinup girl. She was jacked, her arms strong and ripped, and she had a prosthetic leg. The author of the book was listed as Whittaker.

"Oh my God, this is yours. That never occurred to me."

"You didn't know how I made my living."

That was true. The erotic-art thing had been quite the surprise.

She flipped through the book. The images were retro with a modern twist, cheeky and fun and hot. The subjects were of diverse genders, ages, races, and body types.

"So when did you start making art?"

Leo peeked at the book in her hands, fond smile on his face. She stared at his lip ring. What would that feel like when they kissed?

"I took a class to teach me how to draw caricatures for tourists. I needed cash, and tourists are easy marks, but then I loved it. I worked a bunch of part-time jobs until I had enough money to go to art school. Took out student loans. Asked my parents for a loan on top of that, which they reluctantly gave me."

Leo's parents had been less than thrilled that he'd taken off for the West Coast to be a musician, and she imagined they had not been happy about art school either. They'd expected him to follow in their footsteps by opening restaurants and hotels and country clubs.

"Did they know this was the type of art you wanted to make?"

"No. But neither did I. Not at the time. They don't understand it, and they don't need to. We're cool now. I paid them back. I visit once a year, and every so often they meet me in cool places."

Rosie put down the first book and picked up the next in the stack. It was also his work, but the cover was a painting. Maybe watercolors? She didn't know her art well enough to be able to say for sure. It was less stylized, softer, and intimate. Loving. The word popped into her head unbidden.

"That one's not out yet," Leo said abruptly. "That book."

"This is beautiful." She traced a finger over the cover. It showed a white man in a shower, his backside on full display. One of his hands was up on the shower wall in front of him, the other was seemingly on his cock. He had dog tags thrown over his shoulder, dangling between his shoulder blades. Everything was this gorgeous washed-out blue color and certain places were marred by water spots as if Leo had been there in the shower with the man and droplets had reached his canvas. "Is this a real person?"

"Yeah." He laughed nervously. "He's my ex."

"Oh. Damn. He's hot."

"He is. He's the only person I've ever loved besides you. You're also hot, by the way. I have good taste."

"What happened between you?" she asked. "Wait, is the story sad? You don't have to tell me sad stories."

"No. It's not sad, exactly. Mal and I were together through two of his deployments. It worked for us because I live on the road, but once he left the military, my schedule wore on us. He started to fall in love with someone else, and I stepped aside to let him figure it out for himself."

Anger rushed through her, fast and hot and totally due to her own issues. "That's awful."

"It really wasn't." He rubbed a thumb over her cheek. They were standing close. She smelled the lemon scent of his body wash. "He didn't cheat on me. He was open with me about his feelings and fears. He still loved me, but I cared about him enough to see that this other person was right for him. More right than me. I loved him enough to let him go, but not enough to fight to keep him."

She narrowed her eyes. "You're a martyr, Leo Whittaker."

"I'm not." He lifted his hands in surrender. "I'm trying to make myself look good. He was lost and struggling after leaving the Air Force, and I wasn't able to be there for him consistently with all my travel. I have a lot of guilt about that, but we've remained close. I care about him."

"You don't need to make yourself look good for me," she said, infusing her voice with a touch of playfulness, trying to lighten the mood. "I saw you naked. You're doing okay."

That seemed to shock a laugh out of him, which

42

made her oddly proud. Maybe Summer of Rosie: Take #7 could be Comedy. Capital *C* to show that she was serious about it.

"The first page is Mal and his partner," Leo said.

Rosie flipped the book open quickly to discover another shower painting, this one of Mal and a bear of a man, both naked and kissing.

"Did they pose for you?"

Leo nodded, his jaw tight. "Sometimes I draw or paint from photos, sometimes I do quick sketches and fill in detail later. I used photos with them before I went back with the pastels."

Ah, pastels. Not watercolors. She studied the print, and Leo fidgeted, bouncing from one foot to the next. He ran a hand through his messy hair.

"What's wrong?" Rosie asked, worried by his discomfort. She felt like she was discovering all these new facets of him—of the adult Leo—and she was greedy for it. She wanted to know everything.

"I'm just nervous about what you'll think." He grimaced. "I couldn't care less what a random person on Twitter says about my art, but it's hard when it's someone I know."

"Well, I think it's one of the most amazing things I've ever seen." She flipped to the next page. It was a print of Leo on his knees with a Black woman standing behind him, her hand wrapped around his throat, tipping his head back. The way Leo had painted himself was almost chaotic and vague, but she was clear and smooth. "This is beautiful."

"Yeah?" He sounded so hesitant.

A lump caught in Rosie's throat. "Yes. Who is this?" she asked.

"Her name is Sunday. She and her husband are camp hosts at a campground in Washington that I frequent. Deepak's on the next page."

Rosie plopped down on one of the bench seats and turned the page, revealing a painting of Leo, Sunday, and a gorgeous man on a bed with pale pink sheets. Both men were pleasuring Sunday—Deepak at her breast and Leo between her legs. She appeared languid and in total control. One of Leo's hands gripped the back of Deepak's thigh.

Both Leo and Deepak were sexy, but Rosie couldn't stop staring at Sunday. At the way she commanded the page. The way she commanded *the men*. They were serving her.

Leo had rendered every part of her body in exquisite detail. Every curve, every shadow, every inch of smooth flesh.

Summer of Rosie: Take #8. Art enthusiast.

"God, I wish …" Rosie cut off her words at the knees. She wished she could be *that* in control. That she could demand pleasure.

"What do you wish, Rosie?" Leo sat down across from her, his eyes no longer uncertain but full of intensity and promise.

She shook her head and turned the page. The next painting was of Dean, the figure-drawing instructor. Her breath left her in a whoosh. Dean was sitting on a chair, wearing zero pants and an open pale denim shirt, his legs relaxed and spread, his hand on a gorgeously large cock, his head thrown back against the dandelion-yellow wall behind him.

Holy shit, was this why Leo owed him a favor? Her whole body flamed in a second flat. She was on fire, and it was good and scary and overwhelming.

"I can sense the care and love in every piece of art in here. You love them all," she said.

"In different ways, but yes. There's a lot of love in that book."

"I'm jealous."

"Because I've—"

"Not because you've been with these people. It's that you *see* them. It's remarkable, the way your feelings come through. I wish someone would look at me like that." She smiled ruefully. "That sounds pretty pathetic, huh?"

"It doesn't."

A hushed silence wrapped around them. They were on the precipice of something dangerous. Rosie wasn't known for running into danger, but she wanted to sprint straight into whatever this was.

"I could do that," Leo said. "Give you that."

"What do you mean?"

"I could draw you. Sketch you. I could do a simple one. All you'd have to do is sit there."

Her heart started to race. She was a kindergarten teacher. There were a million reasons why she should not pose for a sexy drawing.

She was definitely going to pose for a sexy drawing.

"It would just be between us?"

"Of course. I'll give you the sketch tonight. It's yours. And it doesn't have to be erotic. It could be you lounging there, smiling at me."

Oh, she wanted it to be erotic, but didn't know how to say that out loud.

She set his book aside carefully. "Okay."

He froze, his hands steepled and his mouth slightly open. "For real?"

"Yes."

He jumped up. "Hold tight. Let me get my sketchpad."

When he returned, she asked, "What should I do?"

"Why don't you find a comfortable position?"

She slipped her sandals off. Then she took a deep breath and dragged her top over her head. She'd worn her sluttiest bra for a reason.

Leo dropped his entire sketchpad. "Oh."

"Is this okay?" Rosie asked, nervousness, excitement, and arousal vying for her attention.

Leo fumbled his charcoal pencil next. "Yeah. Fuck. Better than okay. Are you sure you're okay with this?"

"Yes."

"Anything else you want to take off?" he asked, his voice rough and deep.

She'd made his voice sound like that. The power of it lit her up.

"No, I don't think so."

"Lie back on the cushions there."

She did, and goosebumps bloomed over her arms. *Speaking of.* "What should I do with my arms?"

He studied her, his gaze lingering on her breasts and abdomen. Self-consciousness threatened to sway her—she was very aware of the years that had passed since Leo had seen her in any state of undress—but this was *Leo.* Her Leo.

"Close your eyes and pretend you're going to lie there and chat with me. Where would you put your arms to be most comfortable?"

She let her eyes flutter shut and breathed deeply for a few seconds before slipping one arm behind her head and letting the other rest at the waistband of her jean shorts.

"You're fucking hot," Leo said as she opened her eyes.

"Really?"

"Yes. You deserved to be worshiped, Rosie."

Leo didn't start immediately, his eyes flickering all over her from head to toe. She felt his gaze as if it were his tongue. He was playing with his lip piercing, biting it and letting it slip through his teeth, again and again. Finally, he huffed and put his pencil to the paper.

"I do this at conventions," he said. "Fast-track commissions. They're normally super stylized. A lady drawn as a sexy superhero. Two men—one as a jacked Santa, the other an elf. That sort of thing. Do you want that?"

The question felt loaded. "Do you enjoy creating the stylized stuff?"

"I love it. It's fun." His eyes swept over her again.

"People expect boldness from me. Bright colors and sharp lines."

She glanced around the trailer. That wasn't at all how he'd decorated. There was a definite boldness to his pastel pictures, but more intimacy and vulnerability too.

"I have no expectations. Just draw it how you want to," she said.

His smile warped into something cocky and warm. "I don't think I've ever been so excited to draw someone."

"Sure."

"I'm serious. My best work comes when I'm connected to the subject, when I can infuse it with my own feelings. I have lots of feelings about being able to do this for you."

He was staring at her hip and that intense focus paired with his words made heat pool between her legs. She tried not to squirm but didn't quite succeed.

He looked up. "You okay?"

"Yes. Sorry."

"If you're uncomfortable, want me to stop, or need to move, let me know."

She laughed softly. "It's none of those things."

"What is it, then?" he asked.

"I'm hot."

"I can get a fan."

"No. Not like that."

He grinned the dirtiest grin she'd ever seen. It was at once familiar and totally new, an echo from her past but rounded out by maturity and self-assuredness.

His focus returned to her hip. "We can talk while I do this."

"I can try." She was dubious she'd be able to concentrate. "Tell me about the control stuff." She couldn't keep the question in any longer.

His breath was speeding up, and hers matched it. He was drawing quickly, the scratch of pencil to paper sending shivers through her.

"I'm not into intense pain, but I love to be put in my place. To be ordered around. To be used. Playfully slapped. It's … freeing, and it turns me on."

She squirmed again, and his smile went wolf-like. She enjoyed hearing him talk about it, but more than that, she wanted to *see* him give up control.

"I haven't had sex that was freeing since … damn, not since you." She laughed at the realization. They'd been awkward and fumbling, but it had been so sweet.

Leo grunted. "That just makes me mad at your ex-husband. You deserve good sex, Rosie. You deserve everything you've ever wanted."

She'd heard her sister talk about what sex could be, what it could mean, and Rosie had always felt as if she was missing something. She liked sex. Orgasms were great. But sex with Landon had been fraught for so long.

"He cheated, and I knew he was doing it."

"You don't have to talk about it."

"Talking exes has to be the biggest mood killer ever. Unless we're talking about your stacked Air Force pilot."

"You're lying there in the hottest sheer lace bra known to man. You could be talking about taxidermy, and I'd still be drooling. I was hard before you started talking. I'm harder now."

Huh. Taxidermy? She'd add it to her list of potential hobbies.

"He said I was frigid. During one of our fights he called me a cold fish."

"Oh, Rosie. That's not true."

"How would you know?"

"Because I have eyes. Because I don't think the same girl that kissed me until our lips bled when we were eighteen could ever be frigid. Because you stripped off your top like a fucking rock star earlier. Because, if I'm being perfectly honest, I have no doubt that you could take control of any and every situation you were put in, and I find that incredibly sexy."

"I'm not so sure." Rosie wanted to believe him, but her confidence had taken major hits in the last few years.

"I am." He stopped drawing and met her eye.

"I want to get off with someone who cares about me. Landon didn't."

"I care about you."

Rosie's heart hammered in her chest. This was the direction she'd been hoping this would go, but she couldn't quite believe it was happening.

"I know you do."

"Ball's in your court, Rosie. What happens next?"

She closed her eyes and tried to slow her breathing. She was wet ... really wet.

She let the sound of Leo's sketching wash over her.

She squeezed her legs together, trying to relieve the ache there. It didn't work.

She opened her eyes. "Keep drawing me," she said and popped open the buttons of her jean shorts. "And watch."

---

LEO HAD NEVER USED his eraser with such glee. He rubbed out the whole area between Rosie's belly button and the top of her thighs in order to redraw it with her hand in her panties.

Leo'd had his fair share of sex. He'd been to sex parties. He'd been more than one couple's third. He'd painted himself having sex, then presented it to the world. He liked sex. He liked it when it was a fun release of tension. He liked it when it was art. He liked it when it was meaningful and moving.

Watching Rosie open her shorts and slip her hand into her panties was one of the most erotic moments of his life. To see her claim control of her own pleasure—it made his whole body flush.

She wasn't sitting still, but he wasn't complaining. His hands were shaking as he sketched the knob of her wrist and the outline of knuckles under the stretched cotton.

She licked her lips. "I want … uh." A misty pink blush crawled up her neck. That was one of his favorite colors—pale pink—but it was a trillion times better on her skin than on his canvas.

"You can tell me."

"Sorry. I don't … get this wet very often. It's unusual. I'm having trouble talking."

God, he wanted to bury his face in that wetness. He wanted to paint her smile. He wanted to lick the sweat out of the hollow of her thighs, the notch in her throat. He wanted to trace the arch of her foot. He wanted to taste the sour cherry on her lips and kneel at her feet until she ordered him to stop.

"You're in charge here, Rosie," he said at last.

A tremble was starting in her thighs. He wished he knew how to convey that on the page in a way that would do it justice.

He drew the plush of her parted lips and the hooded heaviness in her eyes as she got closer to orgasm.

"Tell me—talk dirty to me," she said, her voice a gasp. "Tell me what you want me to do to you. Give me some good shit to jill off to."

He laughed, and a smile flashed across her face. This was fun.

It also wasn't lost on him the way she'd phrased that. She wanted to know what she could do *to him*, rather than the other way around.

"I'd love for you to order me to jerk off, but not let me come," he said. She writhed, which caused a lock of hair to fall over her cheek. He added it quickly to his sketch before she blew it out of her face. "How would you feel about slapping me?" he asked. "Open palm. Not hard, but on my cheek. You can slap me anytime during sex. Free pass, right here."

"Oh God." She dropped her other hand to her nipple, losing the pose, but Leo didn't give a flying fuck. She was dynamite, and he was lucky to be witnessing this slow-mo explosion.

"What about fucking me, Rosie Posey?" he said sweetly. Her toes curled. Her toenails were painted red and blue, alternating, which was a touch of quirkiness that thrilled him. "I've got a boot box full of dildos, honey. We could sixty-nine. You fuck me with one of those babies, and I lick you until you cream on my face."

"Oh no. Keep going … I'm close."

He set his sketchpad aside.

"You could ride me. A hand on my throat, holding me down. Use me like a fuck toy. I'll service you like it's my calling. Like it's what I was made for. Like my pleasure doesn't matter, only yours does."

She stared straight at him. Her mouth dropped open. The muscles in her legs and stomach clenched and held. Then she moaned in relief, a shudder running the length of her gorgeous body.

He was on his knees at her side before he'd even thought about it. He ripped open the fly of his jeans and delved his hand into his briefs, grabbing his prick. It was so hard it ached.

He pressed his forehead to her hip and whispered, "Please, please."

He felt her shift as she removed her hand from her panties. She used her wet fingers to tip his chin up so she could look at him. She didn't say anything but pressed the same fingers to his lips, and he sucked them down like her slickness was the only sustenance he would ever receive. They were soaked. Her taste triggered a detonation inside him. He whimpered, because it was sudden, too sudden, and he wasn't sure she wanted him to come yet, but he couldn't help it. He shot into his palm, coating the inside of his underwear.

"Good boy," she said gently, her other hand coming up to stroke his hair.

One thing was for certain—she was not a cold fucking fish.

## Chapter Four

———————

Rosie rolled her head against Leo's thigh, reveling in the shift of his muscles and the scritch of his body hair against the back of her neck. He'd cleaned up and changed into new boxer briefs before settling onto the bench seat with her. The blinds were open behind them, and sunrays snuck through, striping their skin with heat.

"Gardening?" Leo asked.

She shook her head. "My brother-in-law has tried. He keeps buying me plants for birthdays and Christmas. He even got me a potted herb garden for Valentine's Day. I keep forgetting to water it." The only plants she'd never accidentally killed were succulents that Perry—Sasha's new husband—had gifted her. Those hen and chicks seemed to be fine with no water at all. She was proud of them. She had rolls of photos of them on her phone.

"Video games."

Rosie paused and thought about that one. It wasn't a

bad idea, except ... "Lots of screen time gives me migraines, but that could work."

"Oh. When did those start?"

"College."

Leo ran his fingers through her hair. He'd been French braiding sections before methodically brushing out the braids with his fingertips. Her hair was going to be greasy as fuck by the end of the afternoon, but it felt too nice to stop him.

"You need a fandom," he suggested. "One with books, TV shows, hot fanfiction, and active argument forums."

"Like what?"

"*Star Wars*, maybe. *Game of Thrones*. I don't know. I don't watch scripted TV and hardly go to the movies."

"But you do watch *un*scripted TV?"

He smiled sheepishly. "I love reality shows. If a contestant gets voted out or there's a panel of judges or it's a race—I'm in. I've auditioned for *Survivor* three times."

Rosie scrambled up onto her knees in order to see him better. "No way. That is awesome."

"Not too awesome, seeing as they won't cast me. I'm guessing they don't want a castaway who draws dicks for a living."

"You do more than that, and you know it," she said. Leo had always diminished his dreams and played up his self-deprecation.

"I do." His voice was serious. He ran a finger, almost absently, over the cusp of her shoulder. The touch made her nipples hard behind the flimsy fabric of her bra. "Thank you."

The hobby thing was a lost cause at the moment. She grabbed his chin between her forefinger and thumb. His whole body stilled. It was exhilarating, the way he reacted to her, to a little forcefulness.

"Those things you said, when you were drawing me—the things you want me to do to you—were you just talking out of your ass, or is that stuff you'd be into?"

His sexy mouth tipped up on one side, his dimple winking. "I wasn't lying."

"I need to make a list," she said. She was practical. She loved lists. Maybe she should admit that her biggest passion in life was stationery and get it over with.

"Hmmm. Kiss me first, Rosie."

She let a smile trip over her mouth. "Ask me nicely."

"*Please*. Please, kiss me." Desperation leaked into his voice. That tenor of need flipped a switch in her.

She clutched his hair in a fist—praise God for his hipster haircut—and tilted his head back before crashing her mouth against his. He gasped, his eyes fluttering closed helplessly. She nipped along his full bottom lip, being rougher than she normally would have been. Leo's body was a small-scale implosion beneath her. He locked tight, his muscles clenching, but then trembles shook through him. She shuffled forward to be fully in his lap and tightened the grip on his hair.

She let her tongue dance over his lip piercing. He whined and opened his mouth wider, so she dove in, taking control of the kiss, of his lips and tongue and teeth.

57

Their kiss tasted of sugary snow cones and her pussy, and it was honestly the hottest kiss of her entire fucking life. His hands were everywhere on her, and her hands were on his throat and in his hair, anchored there. It was amazing.

Landon had never kissed her like this.

The thought jarred her and set off a burst of panic in her chest.

She hadn't kissed another man in years. She hadn't kissed anyone since Landon, and she was so pissed that he was anywhere near her brain. She pulled back.

Leo gazed up at her with a dazed expression. "You okay?"

"Yeah. I was too in my head. I'm sorry."

"Hey." Leo reached up and cradled her face between his palms. "No apologies."

She nodded and turned her head to kiss his palm. She had all these *feelings* pushing at her. Her chest was tight and her pulse fluttery. Her brain felt like a Roman candle, shooting off emotions in blazing fireballs before they fizzled out, unnamed and unrealized. At the forefront was love, but she had no idea if it was legitimate. Did she really *love* Leo Whittaker?

She'd loved him at eighteen. Those feelings had faded into imperceptibility, but they were currently rearing their ugly heads. Was it *love* love, though, or just an echo of it? She was worried that she was simply vulnerable, and this was the first time a man had been kind to her in forever.

Love had never done anything for her except leave her in the dust, choking on fumes. Leo had been the first but not the last. No reason to trust her emotions now. No reason to have them.

It didn't matter much. This thing between her and Leo was nothing but a six-day-long fuckfest (if she had her say).

"List," she said. "List now, kissing later."

Leo's eyes were full of soft understanding, which was embarrassing. Rosie crawled off his lap, and he retrieved a pad of paper and a pencil. Not the ones he'd used to sketch her. The picture of her was on the other bench seat. She was ignoring it. She wasn't ready to see it yet.

"Okay, Rosie. Hit me with your list."

She stared up at the pale wood ceiling. "I want to order you to jerk off and have complete control of when you come." Leo laughed and scrawled it down. She continued, "I want a sex toy free-for-all. We can dump our toys out on the bed and go to town on each other."

"Mmm, yes."

"I'd love to have sex in public, but that's scary to me. It's irresponsible. I'd be fired so fast if I got caught."

Leo chewed on the end of his eraser. "We might be able to figure out a way that feels dangerous but isn't. Let's not count it out, but we'll make sure we aren't putting you at risk."

"Thanks."

"I'd do about anything in the world you wanted. You get that, right?"

"I don't want you to do anything you don't enjoy," she said.

Leo smiled and a ruddy blotch painted both of his

59

cheeks. "Things I don't enjoy? Tickling? I'm pretty easy. I don't love paddles or whips, but I also don't hate it, so we could try it." He scratched the back of his neck. "I think, with you, my main request would be that we communicate and that you don't leave immediately after sex. I want you to use me like a fuck toy, but I don't want to actually be just a fuck toy. Does that make sense?"

Rosie's heartbeat skipped. She'd been gaslit by Landon for so long, about his emotions and her own, that having an open conversation about boundaries and feelings was a revelation.

"It does."

"What don't you like? Anything I need to know?" Leo asked.

She had to think about it. She knew that sometimes she couldn't come without a vibrator, but if she were worked up, she'd pop as easily as a balloon. She knew that she was very interested in exploring this power dynamic between them, but only in bed. She had no interest in anything too hardcore.

"If you're going to fuck me, there has to be some preplanning," she said.

"I can be a planner. Any reason why?"

She schooled her expression. This had been an iffy issue with her and Landon in the past. He hadn't understood. "I get urinary tract infections easily after sex. Not every time, but often. It happened for the first time when you and I were together."

That was thirteen years ago, but Rosie still remembered having to explain to the doctor that the sex seemed to prompt it. She didn't realize at the time that it was a common issue.

"Okay. What can we do to mitigate it? We don't have to have P-in-V sex."

"No!" Rosie's vehemence made them both laugh. "I want to if you want to. I have antibiotics I take after sex to prevent infections, which means we can't do it if I don't have them with me. Oh, and they make my birth control less effective, so we have to be diligent with condoms."

"Which we'd do anyway."

"Exactly."

"Easy as pie. If you don't have your pills, you fuck me, or I go down on you until you drown me, or we use toys, or mutual masturbation, or dry hump, or—"

"Okay, mister. I get it. You know lots of ways to get off." Rosie stretched her arms over her head and popped her back.

Leo grunted. It felt good being there with him, half-naked and comfortable. She didn't have to put on a show but was also very aware that Leo was watching her like she was pay-per-view porn. Maybe it was weird, but the way he was objectifying her was a huge turn-on.

"What else for your list, Rosie Posey?"

She rolled her eyes at the nickname but thought seriously about his question. "You know you can veto any of these?"

"Yep."

"And that some might be logistically impossible?" That was already the case with public sex, but she had no idea how to organize her next idea, which was a blow to her ego. She was an astounding organizer.

"I know. I can tell you've got a brilliant idea in that head of yours. What is it?"

"I want to have a threesome. Or foursome. Or something. Like with more than one person."

Leo's smile sizzled. "Oh, that can be arranged."

## Chapter Five

-------------------

Leo was still in a daze when Rosie left that afternoon. She forgot her sketch but remembered her sex list. Leo put the sketch in the loft in his bedroom where he was currently storing his art.

That evening he pulled it out to add detail to it. Small flushes of color with his colored pencils. A sun stripe on her shoulder.

The next morning, he studied it again. It filled him with the bright sunny summer feeling he got in very specific circumstances. A hot night with barbecue smoke in the air. Cold lemonade on a parched tongue. The juice of a watermelon sticky on his fingers. The scent of chlorine and popsicles. The white-hot magnesium glow of a sparkler.

He took out his sketchpad and idly doodled while he waited for his coffee to brew. He had a meeting with Robin Erco and Sasha Holiday to discuss the pop-up shop. It would be weird to see Sasha after his interlude with Rosie. He had no idea if Rosie would tell her.

An hour and a half later, Sasha greeted him with, "So … heard you went full *Titanic* on my sister yesterday."

"Excuse me?" Leo said, some Midwestern-flustered niceness slipping into his voice.

"You know, Jack painting Rose before banging in a Renault Towncar? Only you were in an RV, and your name is Leo, so—"

"God, Sasha. Filter, please," Robin Erco said with a laugh.

Leo wasn't coy about the shit he did, especially the sex he had, but facing Rosie's brash younger sister was making him shy.

"Oops. Wrong foot, that's me. Hi, I'm Sasha Holiday, head of marketing for Lady Robin's. We've spoken via email, and you evidently had a secret love affair with my sister a decade ago that I didn't know about until brunch this morning. Nice to meet you."

Sasha and Rosie seemed similar at first glance. Both blonde with short hair, blue eyes, and fey-like features. But their smiles were worlds apart. Sasha's was impetuous and a little mischievous, while Rosie's was reticent and sparing.

Leo shook Sasha's hand. "Leo Whittaker. Nice to meet you." He hugged Robin. She looked gorgeous today in a leather pencil skirt and a crisp white sleeveless top that popped against her dark tan skin. Very boss lady. They were old friends, and he had an important question to ask her later. One that was not appropriate for Sasha's ears.

They were in Robin's office, which was sleek and modern with lots of gold embellishments. He was into it. It matched Robin's femme fatale vibe.

"Let's hit the easy bits first," Robin said. She was very take charge. That was one of the reasons he got along with her so well. "The Lady Robin's Independence Day Pop-up Party is on July third. It runs all day, and we're on track to display your art."

"Yes. How many pieces can I display again?" he asked. He had that info buried in an email somewhere, but he couldn't remember.

Robin directed the question to Sasha. She pulled up a chart on her iPad. "We have enough hanger thingamabobs for ten, but that will also be limited by the size of your pieces. If they're huge, I'd say we might only be able to get five in the space."

"None of them are huge," he said.

When Robin and Sasha had first approached him about selling art and his coffee table books, it had been because they'd shown interest in his stylized stuff—his *Characters* collection—but then Robin had discovered that his book, *Lovers*, was set to release the day of the pop-up shop. They'd agreed to make it a launch party/signing.

He didn't make a big stink when his books released because, if possible, he'd already had a gallery show for the collection. He viewed his books as conference and convention bait, but Robin and Sasha seemed to disagree. Per their emails, they wanted him to sell some of his more patriotic or ironically All-American stuff from *Characters*, but other than that, he had free rein.

They got the important details hammered out—what time he could arrive to hang his art, how many books they'd ordered, pricing. Then they discussed the sexy steampunk promotional art they'd hired him to create. It was in his wheelhouse, and his mind was already running away from him. Gears, where the cogs were butt plugs. A man in Victorian dress but showing lingerie underneath. A steampunk warrior woman armed with an arsenal of dildos. He loved these types of projects.

The meeting wrapped up, and Sasha, who had warped into an uberprofessional marketing badass about halfway through, grinned and said, "Want a lube sample?"

"What?" He kept expecting Sasha to be like Rosie, but she wasn't at all.

"I gave some to Rosie yesterday. We named it Slick and Slide." Sasha pulled a bottle out of a bag at her side and handed it to him. He took it with a smile. He sure as hell wasn't gonna turn down good lube.

"Thanks."

"You're welcome. Test it on your wrist a few hours before use to check for allergic reactions. And be nice to my sister. Oh! And that's water based, so it's safe for use with toys."

He ignored the lube talk and said, very seriously, "I will be."

He intended to keep that promise. He and Rosie might not be a long-term match, but his heart was full of her. He couldn't imagine hurting her. As long as they communicated and were on the same page, he didn't see why the next five days wouldn't be a-fucking-mazing.

Sasha gave him a warning stink-eye and a big smile before exiting Robin's office.

Once Sasha was gone, Robin leaned back in her throne—uh, leather desk chair—and arched an eyebrow. "So, Rosie Holiday, huh?"

That expression, that eyebrow, had made him hit his knees in the past. Today, it made him spill the beans.

"I loved her once."

"How the hell did I not know that you used to be in love with my head of marketing's older sister? I'm friends with Rosie too."

He bit his lip and turned his attention toward the window on the other side of the room. Robin had the ability to strip you down with her eyes. He felt off-kilter.

"I didn't know Sasha worked for you until I got the emails from her about the pop-up party, and we'd never crossed paths at conventions. Plus, Rosie was married. I never expected to see her again. It's not like you tell me about your long-lost loves."

"Oh, I don't have any of those," Robin said coolly but with a playful tilt of her lips. He was not good at reading Robin, so he had no idea if what she'd said was true.

"Can I ask you a question? It's inappropriate, so if you'd prefer I wait until you're not at work, I can."

Robin glanced at her watch. "Consider this my lunch. What's up?"

"Rosie and I are hooking up while I'm here. It's a no-strings thing but not quite that simple."

"I gathered."

"Right. So. She wants to have a threesome. Or, at least, generally, have sex with more than one person. Conceivably, there could be more than three."

A tiny glint of excitement flashed through Robin's eyes. "Go on."

He gestured kind of impotently. "Know a way to arrange that, Oh Great Orgy Master?"

Robin laughed. "I might be having a Fourth of July barbecue that could devolve into something interesting. Does that sound like an event you and little Rosie Holiday might be into?"

"Yes. It does." He knew Robin would come through. He'd been to parties at her house before. Interesting was an understatement.

"Both of Rosie's siblings will be there with their part-ners, but they usually leave before the debauchery begins. I'm not lying about it being a barbecue. We will barbecue before we orgy. BYOM. Bring your own meat. Also fireworks."

"Wait. Do I really need to bring meat?"

She laughed. "No. I was just being weird."

"You succeeded."

Robin fixed him with a slightly predatory glare. "Invite Dean. He's a good kisser. I wonder if Rosie is a good kisser. Maybe I'll get to find out."

Leo's heart rate spiked. "Maybe you will."

ROSIE'S patriotic fruit basket looked like a kindergartener had painted it, and she would know. She was a connoisseur of the art of five-year-olds. It wasn't that she'd expected to be a pro as soon as she picked up the paintbrush, but she'd hoped it would at least be fun rather than stressful. Maybe it would have been fun if the community center had served wine like those paint and sip places, or mimosas, to account for the time of day.

Whatever. Painting was not going to be her newest passion. That was okay. She still had the whole hot-sex-with-Leo thing going for her. It would be fleeting, but maybe that was exactly what she needed to catapult her into a new frame of mind when it came to sex, intimacy, and relationships. Sasha—who until a year and a half ago had been the casual-sex queen, God love her—had been telling Rosie for ages that she needed to get back up on the old sex horse again.

However, this thing between Rosie and Leo wasn't *casual*. It was impossible for her to feel casual about him. She felt realistic about him. She felt pragmatic. They would have fun with each other for less than a week, then he'd drive off into the sunset with his RV. She would be left behind with nothing but sexy memories and probably a broken heart.

Holy shit, what was she doing? Besides having a mild panic attack about her high school sweetheart while eating pistachio ice cream in her underwear.

Was this whole agreement a massive mistake?

*Maybe.*

Was she going to milk it for a handful of good orgasms and hope it didn't obliterate her afterward?

*Definitely.*

Her phone buzzed on her coffee table. It was a group text with her siblings.

Sasha: *Bitch, you did not tell me that your virginity taker was a stone cold fox.*

Rosie groaned. She'd given Sasha most of the dirty details this morning. She'd been too excited about it, and the safest person to tell was Sasha.

She would have preferred *this* conversation not include their menace of a younger brother, however. Benji had recently turned twenty-five, was in one of the healthiest relationships she'd ever witnessed, and had a job he loved, but Rosie still saw him as a boy who needed his oldest sister.

Benji: *Ummm, excusez-moi? Rosie finally lost her virginity?*

Rosie: *Please tell me you weren't weird when you met him, Sasha.*

Benji: *Wait a minute? How cum Sasha got to meet some hot mystery ex?*

Benji: *Come**

Benji: *That was an unfortunate autocorrect.*

Sasha: *I can assure you, I am never weird.*

Benji: *I'm so jealous. This is unfair.*

Rosie: *How was the meeting?*

Sasha: *It was good. He's going to make us awesome raunchy*

*promo art, and I'm excited for the pop-up shop. His shit is gonna sell!*

Benji: *He's an artist? What medium? What is his stuff like?*

Sasha: *I gave him lube.*

Rosie: *Oh my God, Sasha! Why? That is so inappropriate!*

Sasha: *No it's not. We sell lube. It was a promo sample. I would have given any visitor to the office one.*

Sasha: *I also told him to be nice to you.*

Sasha: *That was less appropriate.*

Benji: *Who the fuck is this guy? Give me his Insta. I wanna look up his art! And his face.*

Rosie: *I'm gonna murder you, Sasha. I can't believe you said that to him.*

Benji: *Hello? Can you see my texts?*

Benji: *Am I even in this convo? Why are you ignoring me? [crying emoji]*

Rosie groaned and tossed her phone to the other side of the couch. Sasha was such a Judas sometimes. After a few seconds, she picked the phone back up, ignored the ten new messages from Benji and Sasha, and dialed Leo.

"Hello, Rosie Posey."

"Why do you call me that?" She had a big, ridiculous grin on her face.

"Because it's cute."

"You are," she said, teasing.

"Oh, I know. I'm cute, and you're a firecracker. You're way out of my league."

Despite the flirting, she didn't think Leo was *cute*. Not with the tattoos and piercings and dark intensity. No. Leo Whittaker was sexy.

"I'm boring and have no hobbies. I'm in the rec league over here. But not the good rec league. The type of rec league where everyone gets trashed in the parking lot before the game."

Leo laughed, deep and smoky in her ear. She wanted to feel that laugh between her legs. On her stomach. Against her neck.

"What's on your mind?" he asked.

She cleared her throat. "I heard you met my sister today. I'm sorry if she made you uncomfortable."

"She didn't. She's a force to be reckoned with, and she gave me lube. I was thinking of testing it out, but decided I'd wait for you."

"Did you, now?"

"Yeah, I did. We should make headway on that list of yours. Time's ticking."

"Okay. I could be into that."

"Should we move this rodeo to your apartment or my trailer?"

She glanced around wildly. Her living room wasn't clean. Empty popcorn bowl, carton of slowly melting ice cream, two bras she'd taken off at some point and left on the couch.

During the school year, she was super diligent about keeping her home spotless, but this summer, she'd backslid. It was so easy to leave empty hard seltzer cans on top of the coffee table and three pairs of flip-flops under it.

Gross, but freeing. She'd been able to settle down comfortably in her own home, and holy shit, was that different than when she'd been married.

"My place," she said, once she realized she'd be able to pick up easily.

She liked the thought of Leo in her space. He'd see more than her boring gray walls and fake granite countertops and pots of succulents. He'd see *her*.

"Text me your address. I'll bring food."

"You're the best. Oh, and Leo?"

"Yeah?"

"Please be ready for me when you get here." Was that too polite? Maybe she should have said, *You best have a boner for me or else.* But that didn't feel like her at all.

"Ready how?"

"I expect you to be hard."

"Yes, ma'am." Leo hung up, and Rosie let out a shaky breath.

Time to put on pants. And tell her siblings, whose texts she'd been ignoring, that she was going to get laid, and they needed to leave her alone. Then she turned her phone off, to be especially evil.

When Leo walked through the door of her condo thirty minutes later, all kitted out in his motorcycle sex-on-a-stick outfit, Rosie almost ripped away the pizza he was holding and grabbed his dick. She saw the outline of it in his jeans. Instead, she very reservedly removed the pizza from his hands, put it on the counter, and slipped a finger through his belt loop to tug him exactly where she wanted him.

She had this chair-and-a-half that she loved. It had been her postdivorce, self-care purchase—a huge, crisp, cream-colored chair with the most luxurious fabric. She pushed Leo to his knees directly in front of it.

"Hold on," she said. He groaned. Then she realized those were the first words she'd spoken, so she wheeled back around, leaned down, and kissed him gently on the lips. He'd shaved that morning, and she caught the summery scent of lemons. It made her mouth water. He kissed her as if he was giving her everything. It was more profound than she was prepared for.

She pulled back and said, "You okay?"

He blinked a few times. "Yeah."

"You'll tell me to stop if you want me to?"

"Of course," he said.

"Cool. Hold on."

She jogged to her room, found what she was looking for, and rushed back. Leo was in the exact spot she'd put him in. She liked that. She liked it so much, and had no idea what it said about her other than that she was bossy.

She lounged back in the chair and placed her prizes beside her. Leo's eyes were full of fire, and it was all for her.

"Take your shirt off for me, please," she said. He flung off his leather jacket and started to rip the T-shirt over his head. "Wait. Slow down. I want to savor this."

He grinned and slowly raised the fabric. His abdomen came into focus first. He was lean and powerful. His hipbones poked out of the top of his jeans, and his body was smattered with small tattoos. Little artsy things. Art deco patterns below his belly button. A continuous-line illustration of a naked woman on his ribs. Hearts and stars and flowers up his midline. Rosie had seen them in vague ways in the self-portraits in his book, but they were bold, black lines in the flesh. She wanted to map them with her tongue.

She *would* map them with her tongue.

As he lifted his shirt higher, he revealed peaked brown nipples and a dusting of chest hair. Desire thrummed in her belly. He got the shirt up and over his head, messing up his hair. The tattoo on the side of his neck extended along the mound of his shoulder and down his bicep before wrapping his forearm and ending on the back of his hand. The ink was dark—a thin, black brush stroke that turned into graceful swirls and birds in flight and finally, on his hand, the words *Life Raft*.

She let her finger trail down the tattoo's path. Leo vibrated under her touch.

"I want to know about this one, but not right now," she said.

"I want to tell you about it. But not right now."

"Shuck your pants and underwear down, but don't take them off." She needed him half-dressed and untidy.

He followed her orders. In the figure-drawing class, she hadn't allowed herself to look, but she wasn't going to let the opportunity pass her by again.

"Oh," she whispered. She reached a hand out. "Can I?"

He nodded, his chest beginning to rise and fall rapidly. His cheeks were red, his lips wet.

She ran a finger over the tip of his cock. He had a few freckles on his dick. She had remembered that, actually.

They'd laughed about it once. He was girthy with a delicious curve that would hit her perfectly if they fucked. It had thirteen years ago, and she suspected he'd learned some tricks since then. His gaze strayed over to her treasure trove on the arm of the chair.

She let out a soft laugh. "See something interesting?"

"Yes."

"You'll have to wait."

He closed his eyes, pain etched on his features, but she knew it wasn't pain. He was having trouble holding on.

She quickly undressed too, shimmying off a pair of dark green linen shorts and a silk tank top. She shouldn't have gone through the effort to put the shorts on earlier. They'd only made it about twenty minutes total. She wasn't wearing a bra, which Leo hadn't seemed to notice until she was there in the flesh.

"Oh fuck," he gasped. "Please let me … do anything."

She shook her head and stripped off her panties. It felt a bit hedonistic to be naked and on display for him. To be lounging back in her big chair like it was a throne and she was a petulant ruler.

He flexed his fingers at his side and sucked his lip piercing into his mouth.

"You ready, Leo?"

"Yeah."

Without further ado, she drizzled her new lube directly on Leo's cock. He gasped and his body clenched.

"Jerk off, but don't come." This was number one on her list, and she intended to make him pony up.

"*Yes*," he hissed. His eyes fell closed. He was so openly, erotically gorgeous. Wet, sticky heat pooled between her legs, and she shifted them open wider so she could touch herself.

Her clit was slick with her arousal, and a gut-punched noise came from her throat. It kept surprising her—how turned on she was with Leo. She'd had a hell of a dry spell, but she suspected that her pussy practically raining when he was in her vicinity was due to more than that.

His eyes snapped open, and he stared at her. He was leisurely moving his hand on his dick.

"Speed up," she said.

He did. His biceps bulged and veins popped on his forearm. Sweat beaded on the bridge of his nose.

"You're so pretty," he said suddenly, his voice loose and hot. "You know that? You're pretty."

She grinned and grabbed the wand vibrator. It was this obnoxious lime-green color, but she loved it as if it were her firstborn. As soon as she touched it to her clit, her whole body jolted. Leo groaned and stopped moving his hand, forming a fist around the base of his cock.

"I didn't say you could stop, Leo Whittaker," she said sternly.

He shuddered and gingerly stroked his fist up his cock. A pink blush bloomed across his chest, and he slammed his eyes shut.

"Harder," Rosie said.

"Oh God, please let me come."

She spread her legs farther apart, slinging one over

the arm of the chair and letting the other dangle to the floor, and worked the vibrator over her clit.

"Not a chance." Waves of pleasure sizzled through her with each pulse of her wand. She used her free hand to gather up her wetness, then, sitting up, she painted it over Leo's bottom lip. He licked it off and growled deep in his throat.

She tumbled back into the chair with a laugh. She liked playing with him.

"You're doing so good," she said calmly. She didn't feel calm at all. That familiar ache was creeping up on her. She lowered the power of the vibration, trying to drag it out. "I had a dream about you last night. For some reason, I stepped on the middle of your chest while wearing a pair of red Mary Janes, and it was so hot."

He nodded. "Rosie, I'm close."

"Don't come yet, hot rod."

His mouth popped open on a groan.

"So, yeah," she continued. It was getting hard for her to talk. "I stepped on your chest and ordered you to come, and your jizz covered the toe of my shoe. Then I sat on your face." His expression was so delightfully pained. "Slow down. Take a breath."

He did, relief rolling off him. His face was sweat streaked and beautiful.

"You okay?" she asked, checking in with him.

"Better than okay."

"Sounds like you need to keep jerking off, then."

His cock was still shiny from the lube. He swept his

pre-come around the head before stroking himself in earnest again.

Almost immediately, he grasped the arm of the chair with his free hand and held on, white-knuckling it. There was something else he could knuckle.

"Touch my cunt with this hand," she said, tapping the one she wanted him to use.

He shook his head. "Oh no. Oh fuck." But he slipped his fingers deep in her pussy. "Oh god, you feel so amazing, Rosie. I can't last."

Her body arched, but she managed to gravel out, "You better last."

He fingered her gently, seeming to revel in the slickness drenching his fingers. He met her eyes. "You smell good."

"So dirty," she moaned. "I love that you're dirty. I can't stop thinking about it, Leo … Not yet, sexy pants. Don't come … I want to step on you. I want to sit on your face. I want to slap you when you're right on the edge."

"Yes, yes," Leo started chanting as soon as she mentioned face-sitting again. His "yes" after the slapping comment was agonized. He was strung tight, his body like a rocket about to launch. Leo let go of his cock, and held his lube-wet hand up. "I'm sorry, I'm sorry. Too close. I'm sorry."

Maybe it was his apology. Maybe it was the way he started fingering her harder. Maybe it was that she'd moved the vibrator just right over the hard nub of her clit. Whatever it was, she exploded. She shattered on his fingers, surge after surge of pleasure hitting her, until her vision wavered and she was hoarse from moaning her head off.

Once she had blinked some focus back into her eyes, she leveled him with a dark look. "Get your hand back on that cock this instant."

She yanked his hand away from her pussy, tossed the vibrator aside, and took his wet fingers in her mouth.

"Oh fuck, Rosie!"

His arm was trembling, his abs taut and clenched. He had a hungry, needy glint in his eyes. He was on the brink, exactly where she wanted him.

She sat up so she was hovering over him. "Not yet, Leo. Not yet. Get close, then pull back. Can you do that for me?" Her voice still sounded prim, but with a huskiness that she hoped was sexy.

"Yes. I'll do anything," he said so earnestly. So desperately. "Please, Rosie."

She could tell he was getting close. His eyes were hooded, his breath thunderous. He was shaking and sweating and struggling. She ran her hand through his hair, tucking it behind his ear, caressing his jaw. He melted into the touch, almost like he was expecting it.

She slapped him, and he clearly had not been expecting it because the impact made him come all over her.

## Chapter Six

Leo fell forward into Rosie's body, pressing his face to her stomach. "I'm sorry. I'm sorry." He kissed away the stripes of come he'd left on her. His skin was buzzing with relief and satisfaction. His face stung in the best fucking way.

"I'm sorry," he said again. He didn't know why he was saying those words. They felt good. It felt good to apologize for coming before she'd wanted him to, and for making her messy with his release, and because he'd loved her once and it hadn't worked and he was so, so sorry. "I'm sorry."

He licked the spunk off the swell of her breasts and the tops of her thighs. Damn, that had been awesome, but he'd basically blasted her.

She was making shushing noises and holding him steady, petting him. He loved to be cuddled after sex, found he needed a bit of sweetness to reorient himself, to fall safely down to earth. But he wasn't done worshiping her yet.

He pushed her back in the chair, shoved her legs apart, and dove between them.

"I'm sorry," he said again before sucking her swollen clit into his mouth.

"Oh my," Rosie gasped, which was such an understatement for how her body quaked against his lips.

She tasted incredible. Bright and fresh. He was too excited to do this cleanly, to be suave and focused. Instead, he ate her like a starving man.

She grabbed onto his hair and hissed out, "Yes, Leo."

Her legs pressed against his shoulders and her back arched. He could tell she was struggling. Close, but not getting there.

He lifted up for a breath. He felt her arousal on his chin. "What do you need, Rosie?"

Her eyes were smashed shut, and she shook her head. "The second ones are always hard."

"That's okay. Does it feel nice? I'll keep going if it feels good."

"Of course it feels good," she said with an eye roll.

"Okie dokie." He rubbed his chin through her folds, following with his tongue, slowing down to savor it. He could set up a tent and live there for the next five days. Everything he needed was right there.

He brushed his lips against her clit, letting his piercing roll over her. Her toes curled, and she humped against his mouth.

"More," she choked out. "Need more."

"Tell me what you need. Let me please you."

Rosy red blazed across her cheeks. "My ass. Play with my ass." She opened her eyes. "If you want. You don't have to. It's okay."

The sudden reticence jarred him.

"Hey now, where did my stern, bossy bitch go? You don't apologize for jack shit, Rosie. You tell me what you require, and I give it to you."

She let out a shaky breath and nodded. "Finger my ass. I'll come. I'm a hair trigger with ass play."

"Mmm, lucky me."

He returned his lips to her clit. He could tell that she'd cooled down in the course of that twenty-second conversation, so he pushed her hard, sucking and licking and pulling her back up to the brink. He used her arousal to lube his fingers. She was so wet and so warm. It might not be enough, but the prospect was too hot not to try.

Once he was slick, he moved his fingers to her ass. He never stopped kissing her clit. He felt her pulse on his tongue. When his slippery fingertip touched her ass, her whole body froze.

She drew in a breath, and he expected her to say, "Please."

Instead, she snapped, "Hurry up."

He pressed against her entrance and slid inside with one slightly rough thrust. He started to lift his head because he needed to see it. Needed to see himself inside her, but she grabbed him by the ears and shoved him back down.

"Don't stop," was her next order, so he didn't. He

sucked on her clit, relishing the taste. Her arousal dripped from her pussy to her ass, giving him enough additional lubrication to finger fuck her like it was his only job. Because it was.

It didn't take long. Maybe three or four hard strokes. Then the walls of her channel clenched around him, and she cried out hoarsely.

He continued to swirl his tongue over her clit until her tremors stopped. She unlocked her legs from around his head and slowly relaxed them.

He lifted his head, and this time she let him. She was naked and flushed and satisfied, and there was sweat between her breasts. Breasts that were honestly God's gift.

"I wish I could paint you just like this," he said.

She gave a low chuckle. "I wish I could let you." Her eyes popped open. "I left my drawing at your RV."

"You did. Are you concerned about it? I won't share it anywhere, but we could go get it tonight if you're concerned. I should have brought it today, but I didn't think about it."

She seemed to run that over in her mind for a few seconds before shrugging. "I'm not worried."

He pressed a kiss to the top of her thigh. He could still taste himself there, dried and sticky. He stood. "Let me get you cleaned up."

She sat up. "Wait. Aren't I supposed to do that for you?"

"What do you mean?"

A flush—one that probably had nothing to do with recent orgasms—traveled over her cheeks. "You know. I boss you around, so it's my responsibility to take care of you after. Isn't that the rule?"

Leo had to blink a few times to track exactly what she was asking. "There are no rules here. We get to do whatever the fuck we want. I want to take care of you. Then I want to sit in that big chair with you on my lap and eat pizza."

Rosie's smile flitted across her face, relief in her eyes. They needed to talk more about this, but first, clean up and food.

A few minutes later, Rosie was wearing his T-shirt and he was wearing his underwear. Rosie was snugged up against the arm of the chair, her legs thrown over his, her head on his shoulder, and a pizza box on her lap.

She hummed every time she took a bite, really relishing the shit out of her pizza, which Leo found incredibly arousing. To be honest, watching Rosie enjoy *anything* would have turned him on. He wanted to give her the world. If she said jump, he'd jump. If she said edge, he'd edge. If she said orgy, he'd orgy. It was that fucking simple.

He leaned in and kissed the back of her ear. She smelled like honey. Her scent was different, he realized. When they'd been teenagers, she'd worn this perfume he'd gotten her from Victoria Secret because they were ridiculous.

He loved the honey, though. He was tempted to lick her. Instead, he breathed her in and said, "So that was very fun."

"It was."

"Did you enjoy bossing me around?"

She tilted her head. He couldn't see her face, not with the way they were sitting.

"I did," she said. "I'm worried I'm doing it wrong, or I'm not doing something I should be. But … it felt right. Like that's how it's supposed to be between us." She set the pizza box on the floor and turned to straddle his lap. "Did I do okay?"

"Yeah, you were great."

"Even when I slapped you?"

Leo couldn't help his grin. "Did you like slapping me?"

"Is it bad to say yes?"

"It's not. I made my desire to be slapped during sex pretty clear, multiple times."

She lightly touched his cheek. He couldn't feel the sting any longer. "I liked it."

There was this odd light in Rosie's eyes. A tenderness that hurt Leo for some reason. It felt familiar, and it felt scary. Five more days. He had five days.

He'd have to say goodbye. He'd lose her. He'd known it from the moment he'd seen her in that figure-drawing class. He'd been blessed with extra time with Rosie Holiday, but he'd lose her again. It was as inevitable as the summer sun.

Too different. Too opposite. The good-girl teacher versus the bad-boy erotic artist. The nester versus the vagabond.

All the reasons this had to end were a flash point in his mind, running on repeat.

This place would never be his home. He didn't have one. The closest approximation was when he was on the road, the wind hitting him through an open truck window, his trailer behind him. It was a million KOA campgrounds. It was the tiny workspace at the front of his trailer. It wasn't there with Rosie, and never would be.

"Hey." Rosie grabbed his hand. "Where did you go?

Leo stared at their interlocked fingers. He had charcoal under his fingernails. Her hand was so clean next to his. So delicate. She rubbed her thumb over the tattoo on his hand.

"Nowhere."

She smiled, but it was sad. "I remember the pensive, distant, navel-gazing Leo. When I was eighteen, I thought it made you so interesting."

He laughed. "But not anymore?"

She paused playfully, leaving him hanging. "You're interesting, but I'm less apt to let you get away with brooding."

"I was just thinking about what it's going to be like in five days when I leave for Memphis. I'm struggling with it."

Rosie's fingers jerked slightly in his, but her expression didn't flicker. "What's happening in Memphis? I didn't know where you were heading next."

"There's a leather convention there, and I'm meeting friends I haven't seen in a while."

"Are they the type of friend you sleep with?" she asked, her voice curious but not jealous.

"Umm. I have, yes. Doesn't mean I will."

Her eyes narrowed, and he felt like he was about to get disciplined. "You don't owe me anything, Leo."

"Huh?"

"You could go out and fuck Dean tonight, and I'd be fine with that. Well, no. I'd want to watch, so I'd be kind of pissed if you didn't invite me. But I'm not your girlfriend. I don't want to be. I know you, and I'm under no illusion that I'm the right person for you."

A hot, angry ball of emotion welled up in his chest. Despite their differences, despite the reasons he knew they would never work, he couldn't help but feel as if Rosie was *exactly* the right person for him and him for her.

"It's not so easy for me to turn my emotions off, Rosie. I get what you're saying, but—"

Rosie was off his lap and across the room before he finished. She yanked off her shirt—his T-shirt. She was fuming. "I am not emotionless." She pulled her own clothes back on and faced him.

"I didn't say you were."

"Yes. You kind of did, Leo." She pushed her fingers through her hair and closed her eyes. "I'm not handling this conversation well."

The words threw him. He felt himself gearing up for a fight. He and Rosie had never fought when they were younger, but they weren't the same people now. He was hurt that it was so easy for her to call this nothing. Even if it was nothing. Fuck.

She faced him. "I'm not emotionless. I'm not cold. I do care. I'm sorry if I did something to make you think I don't."

"Oh." The ache of anger inside him imploded in a snap. "Rosie."

She laughed sharply. "Don't look at me that way."

"What way?"

"Like you feel sorry for me. Put some pants on. This conversation isn't fair if I have to stare at your package."

"You could try not staring at my package."

Rosie glared. "Where's the fun in that?"

"I don't think you're cold, Rosie Posey. I think you're amazing. And it's gonna hurt to leave. There. That's all. I know you think this doesn't mean anything, but——"

"It means something." She scowled, and she was so perfect it was almost painful.

"I don't want to lose you again."

"You won't." She said that with such confidence. Leo had no idea where it was coming from.

"How?"

She put her hands on her hips. "You have friends in every city, don't you? A lover in every port?"

That same sense of dread began to build in his stomach. It wasn't untrue. He had a lot of friends who would take a tumble with him if the mood hit. He was never hurting for partners, but he probably fucked around far less than she thought.

"I guess."

She smiled wryly at his answer. "Then I'll be that."

Under a no-strings, fuck-buddy arrangement, Rosie would be lost to him for most of the year. He wasn't sure he could live with only brief tastes of her—tempting him, drowning him—before she pushed him out the door and on his way. Yet, that was the fate his lifestyle had destined him to.

"You want to watch me fuck Dean?" he said finally.

Her cheeks turned the color of wild roses. "If you'd let me."

## Chapter Seven

"I made this kite myself. It's called a Rokkaku," Benji said.

Rosie glanced up at the pink kite her little brother was flying. It was a shade darker than the sky currently melting into the late summer sunset. She was jealous of him. Benji and his hunky older boyfriend, William, had started making kites back in the spring after attending a program at the library, which was so ridiculously adorkable she could hardly stand it.

It wasn't fair. Benji attracted hobbies like mosquitoes to perfume. He collected lingerie. He renovated classic cars. He made kites. She couldn't catch a hobby to save her life.

Earlier that day, Leo had gone back to his RV after an hour of cuddling and pizza. He undoubtedly had things he needed to do, but her irrational side worried that he'd left because of that horrible postsex conversation.

Rather than freak out at home about it, she'd

informed Benji that he needed to spend more time with his older sister and had invited herself on Benji and William's kite date. Which was pathetic, but there she was.

They were at a big green space near William's downtown penthouse. The large stretch of manicured grass was ringed by Bradford pear trees and parallel-parking spaces. It smelled like summer—grass and heat and sizzling concrete.

"Here, Rosie. You try," Benji said. He was wearing stupidly short shorts and a tank top with Rue McClanahan's face on it.

Rosie glanced at William, who was sprawled out on a picnic blanket next to her. He was watching Benji with such happy indulgence. It made a weird swirl of emotion catch in her throat: relief and joy and envy.

She stood and took the kite spool from Benji. A soft breeze lifted the kite higher in the air, and she smiled.

"You're a natural. Hold that while I go make out with my man." Benji smacked a kiss on her cheek and skipped off to William. She rolled her eyes but gave them some privacy. She had crashed their date, after all.

The tips of the kite twinkled in the dimming light, and she wondered if Benji had put glitter on it. She let the evening wash over her. The lift and pull of the kite in her hands, the sound of kids playing tag, the chirp of crickets, the warm air, and the pop of firecrackers a few streets away. It was almost meditative, which made it way too easy to think back to her time with Leo.

Everything with Leo had felt so right and so wrong at the same time.

When she'd been with Landon, her emotions during disagreements had been on a short fuse. She'd had to teach herself to keep them in check, which had led to a vicious cycle of her being emotional, then cold, then emotional. More ammunition for Landon to use against her. No matter what she'd done, it had been wrong.

Now, it was hard not to let every fear, every slice of anger, every insecurity rush forward as soon as things stopped going her way.

Maybe she wasn't ready for this. For feelings.

She'd thought she would be okay if she put boundaries in place. She'd thought if she repeated, "This is not forever. This is sex with a guy I care about. He will never stay. This will not be permanent," she wouldn't end up hurt.

Leo insinuating she was hiding her emotions had hurt.

After she and Landon separated, she'd pretended to be unaffected in front of everyone, even the other schoolteachers who had witnessed Landon not-so-secretly court a fresh-out-of-college second-grade teacher—a woman who was now his wife. Sasha had told Rosie to stop bottling up her pain. To share it before it ate her up inside.

Was this one of those moments she should share?

She peeked over her shoulder at William and Benji. She was friends with William, and Benji was fairly emotionally intelligent for a twenty-five-year-old dude. She could talk to them.

They were lying flat on their backs, holding hands and staring at the sky.

She wasn't ready to face her issues yet. She was pretty sure anyone with half a brain would tell her that sleeping with Leo was a mistake. If she was this torn up over three orgasms, then he was not the man she should be having no-strings-attached sex with.

But those had been the best orgasms of Rosie's life. They'd lifted her up, held her suspended in perfect pleasure. Made her rethink what she knew about herself. What it meant to be a match, to fit together with a partner. The pink kite danced in a gust of wind. She watched it rise and rise and rise before swooping suddenly as the wind stopped. She gasped in horror as the kite took a nosedive and crashed into the grass.

She stared at it, not sure the extent of the damage. Tears sprouted in her eyes. What the fuck was wrong with her?

"Hey, Rosie!" She turned toward Benji's voice, ready to apologize for letting his kite hit the earth so hard, but he seemed unfazed. "I'm gonna get us hot dogs. Want one?"

She'd already had pizza, but a hot dog sounded fantastic. She nodded.

Benji grinned. "Be right back." He jogged off, evidently in pursuit of food. There must have been a sidewalk vendor nearby.

William stood and approached her. He was wearing gym shorts, flip-flops, a crisp blue T-shirt, and a ball cap. He looked like a hot little-league coach, honestly.

"Want me to help you get the kite back in the sky?" he asked.

"I didn't break it?"

"No. This kite's made of sturdier stuff than that, Rosie." William took the spool from her and got the kite up within a minute.

They both watched as it bobbed in the breeze. There was hardly any daylight left, and lightning bugs had started to blink under the Bradford pears.

Rosie had always liked William. He didn't say much, so when he spoke, it was important. He'd been married to his work until he'd met her brother. Now she was pretty sure he'd one day be married to Benji. If that were the case, she'd majorly lucked out in the brothers-in-law department.

"Benji told me you're dating an eighteen-year-old," William said, a sly smile on his face. He handed her the spool.

"What?" She narrowed her eyes, and he laughed. "I'm not *dating* anyone, but I have been seeing a man I knew when we were both eighteen. He's my age. Benji is such a little shit."

"A loveable one, though."

"True." She rolled her eyes.

"So how is dating going? Oh, excuse me. How is *seeing* a man you knew at eighteen going?"

She ignored his gentle teasing and bit her lip. Then she blurted, "I'm going to crash and burn, William. I'm in over my head."

He stared at her thoughtfully for a few seconds. "I think you're made of sturdier stuff than that."

---

ROSIE COULDN'T STOP THINKING about William's words. They followed her through her hot dog, insomnia, and a lazy morning the next day. No hobby search today because she was working a shift at a fireworks stand from four in the afternoon to ten in the evening. It was a fundraiser for the local teachers' association. They did it every year, and normally she enjoyed it. But today, working there meant she might not get to see Leo, as he was spending the morning golfing with his father.

*Golf.*

She couldn't imagine a world where Leo Whittaker held a golf club that wasn't meant for smashing something, but there they were.

Still, she'd gone to her shift to sell fireworks prepared for a late-night booty call. She had an overnight bag in her car. There were benefits to being a super planner.

The fireworks stand had hit a lull by seven, and they only had one customer. Unfortunately, he was a jerk.

"Which of those firecrackers is the loudest?"

Rosie gave a tight-lipped grimace to the middle-aged white man in front of her. He was ruddy-faced and seemingly jocular, but in a way that set her teeth on edge. He'd already asked her which firecracker had the "best scent" and the "most exciting *peak*." Rosie didn't get paid enough for this.

Actually, she wasn't getting paid at all for this.

"I'm sorry. I don't know," she said.

"Well, you work here, don't you?" He grinned. "Maybe you should."

"This fireworks stand is a week-long fundraiser for the school district's teachers' association. I'm a kindergarten teacher." Several signs—on the nearby road and the stand—advertised the teachers association and asked for support for local educators. She figured it would be obvious that "fireworks saleswoman" wasn't her full-time job, but perhaps not.

She pointed out the bricks of flashlight crackers and M-80s. "These all go bang."

She tried to focus on the things she liked about working the fireworks stand rather than the things she didn't—i.e. customer service. She loved the smell of flash powder and cheap paper. It reminded her of summertime —of Benji as a child, playing with sparklers in the parking lot of their apartment complex, a maniacal grin on his face, and Sasha running through a sprinkler to keep cool. Good childhood memories. Shiny summer ones. She didn't have a ton of those.

"Anything I can do to convince you to come to my party?" the man asked, snapping her out of her memories.

"Nope, sorry."

This was the second time he'd invited her to his Fourth of July party. She didn't have Independence Day plans yet, but she figured they'd involve her clit and Leo's mouth. Woo, patriotism.

Her plans definitely wouldn't be with this bastard.

"What's your favorite of the bigger canister shells?" the man said. "Maybe if I buy it, you'll come."

She gestured to one of the most expensive fireworks in the stand. "The Big A-Hole is very popular. It's only two hundred dollars."

"What's it called?" he asked, squinting in the direction she'd pointed.

"The Big Hole."

Her coworker, Tyler Vlachos, snorted. Tyler, a special education teacher at her elementary school, sent her a searching look as if he were asking, "Want me to step in?" Rosie smiled at Tyler to show him she was fine.

Tyler wore Hawaiian shirts every day, even in the winter, and was currently sporting black socks with his sandals. He was a *Jeopardy* winner and one of the funniest people she knew. She adored him.

"There's that smile I've been waiting for," the customer said. "You're prettier when you smile."

She mean-mugged him before grabbing two large variety packs and smacking them on the wooden counter. "Variety packs are buy one, get one free. They have everything you'll need for your party."

"Okay."

"And I don't smile for men who can't take a hint. I laugh at them."

The man's eyes went dark, but he huffed and threw

down forty dollars. "No need to be snippy about it." He snatched the variety packs and stormed off.

Rosie gathered up his money and happily put it in the cashbox. "I'm surprised he bought anything."

Tyler grinned. "I eternally remain in your thrall, my work wife."

"You couldn't pay me enough to take another trip down matrimony lane, but you do make it tempting, Tyler."

"We'd be so poor."

A laugh burst out of her. "True."

Rosie sat on the counter, choosing a spot where she could see Tyler and any approaching customers. The stand's plywood walls and particle-board awning were no match for the late afternoon sun, and Rosie fanned herself with a ledger book.

Earlier, Tyler had bitched about the lack of support from administration in his special ed classroom. And she had bitched about the fact that she would have to purchase all the new puzzles, art supplies, and early reader books for her kindergarten classroom. Teacher stuff. It was a rocking good time.

As easy as it was to complain, she was thankful for her school. Until the previous school year, she'd been working in the same building as her ex-husband *and* his new wife. It had been untenable. The district had moved her, and she was content. She liked her job, her students, and her coworkers. Contentment was a fickle beast, though.

"What do you do for fun?" Rosie asked Tyler. He was

goofily grinning at his phone. She could see he was on a dating app.

His head snapped up. "I'm sorry?"

"What do you do outside of work? What are your hobbies?"

He scratched his chin. "Besides trivia?"

She smiled. "Yes, besides that."

"I'm in a Scrabble club."

"Really?"

"I'm the youngest there. I'm not that skilled, but it's fun to be around the other members. They try to set me up with their grandsons. One of these days, I'm gonna get a date out of the deal."

Rosie's mind snagged on something he'd said. It wasn't the activity he enjoyed but the people. She hadn't thought of that. She'd been searching for hobbies, but maybe she should have been searching for community instead.

That felt a bit too daunting, to be honest. She hadn't had a lot of consistency in her life. Her parents were flakes. Her ex-husband was a gaslighting cheater. Even Leo had left her. The only dependables in her life were Sasha and Benji.

She didn't trust people. She needed to rely on herself. It was up to her to find security and happiness. She couldn't put that on anyone else.

Rosie and Tyler spent the next few hours chatting about their coworkers, analyzing Tinder profiles for Tyler, and helping people spend obscene amounts of money on fireworks.

By nine thirty, their steady stream of customers had completely abated. June bugs and moths kept swooping in and knocking into the stand's two indoor lights, both unadorned yellow bulbs.

Her phone lit up with Leo's name.

"Oh. Who has your face all aglow like that?" Tyler asked.

"A friend. Or, I guess, an old boyfriend."

Tyler propped his chin in his hands and grinned. "What did he say?"

She opened Leo's message.

Leo: *I've missed you today.*

She hated the way that made her heart melt.

Rosie: *You too.*

Leo: *I'm about to leave my parents' house. Are you at the fireworks stand?*

Rosie: *Yes, until 10.*

Leo: *Where's it at? I'll stop by and say hi.*

Leo's parents lived in a fancy gated community a few minutes from Boone's Nursery and Tree Farm, which was where the fireworks stand was parked for the week. Or, at least, that was where his parents used to live. She had no idea if they'd moved in the intervening years she'd been out of touch with Leo. That neighborhood had been full of old money and country club memberships. When they'd been teenagers, she would park her grandma's Ford Tempo in the ditch by the gate and wait for Leo to sneak out to see her.

She gave Leo the address, and he told her he'd see her soon. She set her phone down and turned to Tyler.

"Hot date?" he asked with a sly smile.

"No," she lied. She didn't want Tyler to tease her. He'd get the full Leo experience soon enough. "He was just saying hi."

"Bummer. I'm behind on my soaps. Thought this might give me my fill of drama."

"Sorry to disappoint."

Not five minutes later, a motorcycle squealed into the gravel lot.

Leo swung a jean-clad leg over the seat to dismount. She loved his body. Not too tall, lean like a swimmer, wide shoulders, and narrow hips. She spotted the tattoo snaking up his neck, peeking over his leather jacket.

Tyler whistled. "I can get this one," he said, sounding dazed.

She stifled a laugh. "Sure thing."

Leo removed his helmet and shook out his dark, wavy hair. He strolled up to the counter, all loose hips and swagger. It was practically porny, like one of those wet T-shirt videos. She was going to memorize that whole sequence and masturbate to it once Leo was off in Memphis banging other people.

"Hey," Tyler said. "What can I help you with?"

Leo smiled at Tyler, then let his eyes wander over to Rosie, locking her in place with his gaze. "I think I've found what I'm looking for."

Rosie laughed. "That was so corny."

Leo shrugged and leaned against the counter.

Tyler's mouth popped open in understanding. "Well, hello, Mr. Motorcycle."

Leo blushed, which Rosie found unbelievably delightful. She could have watched Tyler flirt with Leo for hours if that was how he was going to react.

"Leo, this is my coworker Tyler. Tyler, this is Leo Whittaker. His parents own Froth and Forage."

"Oh! My ex loved that place," Tyler said.

"But not you?" Leo asked.

"Nah. I'm not into that swanky stuff."

Leo chuckled. "Me neither, man." He cleared his throat. "Actually, I might have Fourth of July plans. Maybe I should buy fireworks, just in case."

"We're here to help," Tyler said.

"You can't transport fireworks on that thing," Rosie said, nodding toward his bike.

"Hmmm. Maybe you could put them in your car and follow me home? Would that be a good compromise, Rosie Posey?" Leo openly eye-fucked her again, and she started to sweat.

"Not if you keep calling me that."

Leo bit his lip on a smile as if he knew she liked the nickname—which she did—but disagreed because she liked to be disagreeable. Also true.

"Should I buy the ones with the coolest names?" Leo asked. "What's that say? Buzzing Bumblebee?"

"One of the variety packs would be my suggestion for a party," Tyler said. Variety packs had been their mantra all day. It was the easiest, most economical choice. "That way you won't have to make a ton of little decisions. These have firecrackers, including snakes, snappers, smoke bombs, champagne poppers, and flashlight crackers as well as fountains and a handful of aerials."

"Variety is the spice of life, huh?" Leo said. "When I was a kid, we played with these fireworks that were attached to a long stick. The stick would direct where the firework would fly. Do you know what I'm talking about? They were fun. Dangerous, though."

"Bottle rockets," Rosie blurted, unable to help herself. She'd always been a relentless know-it-all. "They're illegal in some states."

"Yeah. You got any of those?" he asked.

"Nope. A redneck bought us out of them about an hour ago," she said.

"I'm not sure if I think that's awesome or terrifying," Leo said.

Tyler was still watching them both, unrestrained glee on his face. He clapped his hands. "I'm gonna start counting the cashbox while you two flirt."

"What do those Alien Invasion things do?" Leo asked Rosie, pointing toward a pile of gray discs.

Rosie leaned her elbows on the wooden counter, bringing her closer to his level. "After you light the fuse, the disc zooms into the air, glows red, and busts open. When it busts, tiny green men fall to the earth." That was a lie.

He grinned. "And the Fried Chickens?"

She glanced toward the bottom shelf where the novelty firecrackers were. "The Fried Chicken lets out a cock-a-doodle-do and drops fireball eggs before exploding." She loved bantering with him. He understood her dryness and humor.

"What about that big one with the camo and American flag?" He squinted. "The Bad Mother Ammo Crate."

It was one of those huge cakes that you lit, and it sent up a bunch of fireworks one after the other.

"The fireworks spell 'douchebag' in the sky. Very pretty," she said.

"And the One Minute Ride?"

"It'll leave you disappointed. A total dud."

"Damn, I fucking adore you," he whispered. He was smiling and seemed slightly out of breath.

She wanted to comb her fingers through his hair. It was sweaty from his helmet. She wanted to grab onto the messy strands and ride him. She wanted to joke and laugh with him. She didn't want this to ever end.

"I'll take those variety packs," he said thickly, pulling a few bills out of his wallet. He handed the money over to Tyler, who added it to his totals. Rosie packed up Leo's fireworks in a paper bag with a handful of punks and handed him her keys. As he put his purchases in her car, Rosie and Tyler continued closing up the stand.

Tyler was the treasurer of the teachers' association, so he was responsible for taking home the cashbox every night. The fact he'd worked this evening had saved him an extra trip.

Rosie was closing and locking the last window—the stand's windows and doors all locked with padlocks—as

Leo made his way back toward them. When he reached the side door, he said, "Can I lock this for you?"

Tyler said, "Sure. Thanks!" before he and Rosie exited and locked the other side.

They made their way to the gravel parking area. Leo walked Rosie to her car, and Tyler gave them a wave before leaving them to it.

Once they were alone, Leo turned to her with what she could only describe as a demonic grin on his face. "You wanna fuck in that fireworks stand?"

## Chapter Eight

"Excuse me?" Rosie said.

"It's kind of like public sex, isn't it?" Leo asked. When she didn't answer, he said, "If you don't want to, I need to go lock that door for real."

Her mind was running a million miles a minute. There was no one around, and Boone's Nursery and Tree Farm was also closed for the night. There weren't any other businesses nearby.

Emotion flashed through her. It was happiness, and it was that recklessness that was so addicting when Leo was around. She closed her car door gently and took off for the fireworks stand without another word.

She heard Leo hiss, "Fuck yes," from behind her.

She pushed open the door that Leo had obviously not locked. It was pitch black inside, but she didn't want to risk turning the lights back on, so she set her cell phone on the counter with the flashlight blazing toward the ceiling. Leo was right behind her. He closed the door and opened his mouth to speak.

"Shush," she said. Then she kissed him.

It was a claiming, hot kiss, one that lit her up inside. His hands groped over her, grabbing her ass and her breasts, like he wanted to touch all of her as quickly as possible.

She was wearing a gingham sundress, so it was easy for him to ruck up her skirt and rip her panties down. He helpfully shoved her underwear into the pocket of his jeans, which she appreciated. It would be horrifying to accidentally leave them there.

His fingers delved between her folds and her back hit the door. She couldn't seem to catch her breath. It was stuffy without the breeze blowing through the open windows, and the scent of fireworks was acrid in her nose. She bit Leo's neck hard, and he groaned and pressed her into the door as if he couldn't stand to be anywhere but against her body.

"Do you have a condom?" she whispered in his ear.

He nodded. "Do you have your pills?"

She nodded. "In my car. Fuck me." She nipped sharply at the soft fleshy part of his lobe. "Hard and fast."

Leo fumbled his pants open and sheathed himself in a condom. He was moving quickly, his body trembling. He seemed eager to please her, to get inside her.

Within a few seconds, he was ready to go. "Should it be sweet the first time we do this?" he asked

"No." She grabbed a handful of his shirt and yanked

him to her. "I don't want sweet. I want you to bang me like a drum. Get. In."

"Oh God." He lifted her leg, planting her foot on a shelf next to a box of champagne poppers. Her back was flush to the door, and she was pinned open. He thrust into her hard.

It was a bit of a stretch. She hadn't had sex in a long time, and normally, when she played with toys, she used lube. But she was wet enough, and the harsh invasion of him felt like the dirty, raunchy sex she'd always craved.

They were the perfect height to fuck standing up, she realized. They fit. They fit everywhere.

Leo was trembling and a broken moan fell from his lips as he bottomed out.

"Hush," she admonished, which seemed to send him into an even greater fever. "Don't make me gag you."

He stifled his sex noises in the sweep of her neck and fucked her into the door with the type of abandon she'd only ever dreamed of. It was frenzied and rough. Her head hit the door as she arched her neck. Sweat dripped down her spine and slicked her skin under his palms.

She fisted the back of his T-shirt and held on. Each thrust was sharp and strong, hitting her just right. Her pussy clenched around his cock and stars burst in her vision. She was close but not quite there. She loved this moment during sex. The struggle to the peak. The delicious aching pain before the release.

Leo sucked kisses on her neck. Then with a move so quick it made her head spin, he ripped down the straps of her dress, exposing her tits. He cupped one of her breasts, leaned down, and snagged her nipple with his tongue.

"Harder," she demanded. She didn't know if she wanted him to be rougher with her nipple or to fuck her harder. Or both.

He did both.

He lifted his head, braced one hand on the wall above her, hammered into her, and pinched her nipple so hard she cried out. He crashed his mouth onto hers to silence her cries, but they were banging into the door pretty loudly. If anyone was around, there would be no doubt what was happening in the fireworks stand.

Heat bloomed through the small of her back and warmth flooded her pussy. Almost there.

She was almost there.

Leo tore his mouth from hers. "Please, Rosie. Please." He was chanting, begging against her skin, his voice so needy and so at odds with the way he was taking her apart.

Her knees started to shake, and she had to smack a hand against the doorjamb to hold herself up. Leo changed his angle slightly, giving his hips a swivel at the end of each thrust, which resulted in extra pressure and drag on her swollen clit.

Her fuse was getting shorter and shorter by the second. He tweaked her nipple, and she ignited.

She came in a shower of sparks and heavy breaths and sharp cries, and he came silently, sucking on her neck like a little vampire, his body a wave she wanted to ride forever.

LEO DIDN'T WANT to pull out. He wanted to stay pressed up against Rosie's body for the foreseeable future. Unfortunately, they were in a sweltering fireworks stand, and he figured they'd about used up all their luck.

He stepped back, but as soon as his body wasn't holding Rosie's in place, her foot slipped from the shelf and kicked a box of snappers onto the floor. Several of the snappers popped, and they both jumped a mile.

He quickly steadied her. "You okay?"

She responded by giving him the most un-Rosie-like giggle he'd ever heard.

"I can't feel my toes, and *I'm wonderful.*" She laughed again. It sounded so free and full of joy.

He kissed her swiftly, then helped her fix her clothing. She was leaning heavily against the door, her breath slowing in increments. She looked satisfied.

He grinned and tied off the condom. "Let's scoot, beautiful."

She sighed and drew him into a gentle hug. "Thank you. This was ... *wow.*"

He pressed his lips to her temple and led her out into the warm night air. She locked the door behind them. There was a trashcan on the far end of the parking lot, and he dumped the condom there.

He met her back at her car and asked, "What next?"

She took her antibiotic and shrugged. "I'm going to pee at the gas station down the street. Then maybe I could meet you at your house. Your Airstream, I mean. I have an overnight bag with me."

Relief rushed through him. Sex in risky locales was great, but it didn't allow for the tenderness he craved afterward. He was glad their night wasn't over.

Within twenty minutes, Rosie was back in his RV, fresh faced and put together. If he hadn't been there, he would never have suspected she'd just been pounded into next week.

She dropped her overnight bag by his front door and kissed him. It felt so normal, having her there, her greeting him as she came in the door. He could get used to it, he realized.

He'd been painting earlier—a continuation of the doodles he'd started the morning after he'd first seen her again—and his workspace was still messy.

"What's this going to be?" she asked, studying his canvas. He'd been playing with watercolors, and the picture hadn't taken shape yet. He was painting by the seat of his pants.

"Haven't decided," he said.

She smiled. "It's colorful."

"I'm into soft colors right now. Pastels. Dean says it's my baby-shower phase."

"What other phases have you gone through?"

"Hmm." He wrapped his arms around her from behind, and she leaned back into him like it was the most natural thing in the world. "I don't know. Up until recently, I'd only done the stylized illustrations. I enjoy that. It makes me good money."

"What made you start gravitating toward this?" she asked, gesturing toward his painting.

He considered that for a long moment, taking the time to bury his face in Rosie's honey-scented hair. He'd been enamored with this new aesthetic for over a year. It had started with a daydream. A memory. He'd been lying in bed, the sun streaming in through his windows, the air glittering with dust. He'd closed his eyes and seen iridescent smoky clouds tinged with pale colors and shimmering water and pink sky. It had stuck with him, that image, and had caused his palms to itch until finally he'd made plans for his *Lovers* collection.

"Nostalgia, maybe?" he said. He didn't want to give too much away. The colors he'd been using weren't trendy. They were dated in a way that charmed him.

She turned in his arms. Her eyes were a little serious. A little too knowing. He felt as if she could flay him open with nothing but a word.

But she didn't. She smiled again—that stingy smile that made him feel like a king—and pressed a quick kiss to his cheek.

"Let's go to bed," she whispered in his ear. "I want to cuddle."

"Your wish. My command." He grinned and swept her into his arms. She gave another of those perfect laughs, so he threw her over his shoulder, ready to storm his bedroom. She whooped. He grabbed her ass. It was magical.

As he carefully walked them through the narrow

kitchen, she said, "Wait! My bag. There are sex toys in there."

He groaned, doubled back, and picked up her bag without putting her down. Once they made it into his room, he dropped her bag and tossed her onto his bed. The bed stretched the whole length of the room, edge to edge. He'd worked hard to make it as cozy and comfortable as possible. The Airstream was his escape—literally as it had wheels—but his bedroom was his refuge. He hadn't allowed many people into this part of his life. He kept it close to his chest, but he loved having Rosie there.

He flipped on his reading lamp before falling into her arms. She snuggled up against his chest. He held her, running his fingers through her short hair, and her body grew heavy against his.

After some time, she asked, "Do you ever feel lonely?"

"No. Not really."

As soon as he said the words, he knew they were a lie. His heartbeat skyrocketed, and the metallic taste of adrenaline flooded his mouth. He didn't understand his reaction.

"I think I'm lonely," she said, while he quietly freaked out. "My marriage sucked, but there are things I miss. Cuddling and having a person to eat meals with. Not special meals, like dates or brunch with my siblings. I mean, eating cereal together because you're lazy and your favorite show's about to start, you know? I miss having someone on the other end of a phone line. I would leave work before Landon, and he would call me on his way home every day to see if I needed anything from the store. I miss that."

"Routines." His voice was strained.

She nodded against his chest. "Yes."

"I've been running away from routine for thirteen years, but I see the appeal."

She leaned back so she could see his face, and her lips tipped up. "I don't think you're running from routine."

"You don't?"

"No. You're not running *away from* anything. You're running *toward* it. Toward experiences. Toward love. Toward adventure. Toward inspiration. I've always believed that."

He'd tried, through the years, to fully explain his impulse to move, to not put down roots, to travel, and he'd usually failed. She'd summed it up in ten seconds flat.

"I think …" He chewed on his lip. This was hard. "I think I've hurt people in the past. Because I run. My parents. You. Friends who wanted to be more. Mal. I am lonely, but I'm also *me*. I don't want to hurt anyone else by being me."

She cupped his cheek. "You won't hurt me by leaving this time. I promise."

It would hurt him, though. That was what he didn't say. He was selfish. His lifestyle sometimes hurt the people he loved, but it also hurt him. It robbed him of connections he craved. It left him lonely, but he had never been able to find a balance between the freedom of the open road and love that lasted. The one time he'd tried, it had ended poorly.

Rosie was seemingly able to compartmentalize their reconnection. To put it in a box labeled "fuck buddy" or "deadline incoming." He admired her for that. He'd been great at that type of compartmentalization for years. He had friends all over the country that he happily screwed around with then left with a smile. It was mutually beneficial. He knew they were on the same page.

The longer this went on with Rosie, the more he was sure they were not on the same page. She was keeping up her end of the bargain. It was his heart that was changing the rules.

Ideally, he'd tell her that. Say, "Hey, I think I could still love you, and this is getting scary for me." But he wasn't gonna do that. He was going to drown himself in her, give her all the experiences she craved, help her fulfill her sex checklist and maybe find a hobby. Then he was going to run away and lick his wounds.

## Chapter Nine

Rosie had said the wrong thing. She could tell. Leo's heart was racing under her palm, and he looked overwhelmed.

She had no idea how to turn this conversation around. Fear and disappointment and guilt pushed at her. A compulsive response she had no control over. It had been hammered into her through the years of her marriage, and she *hated, hated, hated* it.

"I'm sorry," she said.

He frowned, and that made it ten times worse. "What for?"

She stuttered before saying, "I don't know. I feel like I messed up."

His expression went thunderous. "You didn't do anything wrong." He rolled on top of her, and her breath left her lungs in a rush. "You don't have to apologize for jack shit, Rosie Holiday."

His body was hard against her, pressing her into his soft bed.

"You're right." She shook her head, trying to clear it. "I'm sorry."

He laughed and bit her neck. "Stop apologizing."

Her skin was tender under his teeth. He'd sucked on that spot earlier when they'd fucked. It felt good, that sting.

"I want you," she whispered.

"I'm yours for the taking."

She pushed him off so she could grab her bag and dump her sex toys everywhere.

"Your turn," she said.

Leo leaned over and retrieved a box from beneath the bed. He dumped his toys alongside hers. He still had that edge of vulnerability in his eyes. She wasn't sure if she wanted it gone or if she wanted to exploit it. To open him up even more. To make him give all that emotion to her.

"You pick," she said.

With a confident grin, he selected a handful of toys, condoms, toy-cleaning wipes, and lube from both their stashes and pushed the rest to the floor. She studied the items on the bed and figured out a game plan on the fly.

She used toy-cleaning wipes and told Leo to take his clothes off. He obeyed.

She loved how well he obeyed. She stripped her dress off. She wasn't wearing any undergarments. Her panties were in Leo's pocket and the dress had a built-in bra. Made for easy fucking.

She picked up a butt plug. It was one of Leo's, a heavy, curved bulb. "This okay?"

His "yes" was a moan.

"Do you need me to prep you first? Fingers or anything?" she asked. She'd never prepped anyone except herself. This was uncharted territory.

"No. I'm fine."

She shoved his legs apart, and he moaned again. His naked body was a masterpiece. Hot, shiny with sweat, corded with muscle. No wonder he painted himself in the throes of sex.

She lubed up the plug and placed it at his entrance, and he started begging under his breath. A litany of "please, please, please."

The gruff cry he made as she pressed the plug in was the sexiest thing she'd ever heard. Once it was seated, she wiggled it a little, and he grabbed at the sheets under him, his eyes rolling back.

*Bingo.*

She laughed breathlessly and moved up the bed. His bed was amazing, and having Leo sprawled out in the middle of those blankets and pillows was a gift.

"Make me wet," she said, her voice ragged. She swung a leg over so she was straddling his face and fisted a hunk of his hair.

He sucked the inside of her thigh. "You're killing me."

"In a good way?" she asked.

"The best way."

He laved over her clit, and her pulse jumped. She

twisted her hips so his chin dragged through her folds, his stubble lighting her up. He clutched her ass and held on.

"Get me ready for you," she said. "I want to be dripping."

He licked her, delving into her pussy before focusing on her clit. Then he repeated the motion, again and again. The slide of his tongue inside with each pass made her toes curl and her stomach clench. It was addicting, but not what she wanted. She needed something weighty. Something hard and blunt and searing to make her come.

"Enough," she said, gasping. He didn't stop. She yanked his mouth off her clit. "Enough." He smiled his take-no-prisoners grin. "Don't be bad, Leo, or you won't get your reward."

"Oh yeah? What's my reward?" he asked. She slid down his body and suckled the tip of his dick, the taste of his pre-come sharp on her tongue. She popped off before he'd had time to react. His eyes were wide and his breathing fast.

She rolled a condom down his cock. "Well, I'm guessing you didn't pick that harness and dildo for bed decoration, did you?" He shook his head. She laughed. "Don't come."

She straddled him again, this time taking his prick inside her with one swift movement. Her body was still relaxed from her orgasm earlier, and her cunt was wet from his mouth. He slid in like he belonged there.

Maybe he did. The thought was a wild rebellion in her brain, one she couldn't quite stifle. It pinged around in there as she started to ride him.

Leo whispered, "Oh my God."

She wanted to get possessive with him. Tell him that he belonged to her. And she belonged to him. And that *this* was right. The connection between them was *right*.

But she didn't do that because it wasn't going to happen. He was going to leave, and she was going to figure out a way to be okay with that. So she held him down, planted her palms on his chest, and tried to lose herself in the sensation of having him inside her.

"Yes, Rosie," he hissed. "Use me." She rode him in long, slow strokes. He was shaking, his fingers digging into the flesh of her thighs.

She grabbed a flat, palm-sized vibrator from the bed. It was the ideal size to hold against her mound and the base of his cock. She turned it on and ground down on it, the vibration dragging against her clit with every swivel of her hips.

"What are you feeling?" she asked.

He was panting, his head tipped back and his muscles standing out in stark relief. "Like I'm ... about to blow."

"Better not." It was getting hard for her to speak as well. His cock was nudging against her G-spot and the vibrator was a perfect wave of sensation against her sensitive clit.

"Fuck. You're beautiful. You can fuck me even if I ... if I—"

"I plan to be inside you when you come," she gritted out. She clenched around him, making her eyes roll back in her head and him cry out.

"Each time you move … the plug. It hits me … It hits my …"

"I know, baby. Hush now and hold this." She moved his hand to her vibrator, instructing him to keep it in place. Then she planted her hands beside his head so she could bounce on his cock.

He closed his eyes, a pained expression on his face. She was positive he wasn't in pain. He was trembling and his cock was rock hard inside her.

She touched his neck lightly, a tease of her fingertips over his Adam's apple.

He gasped and opened his eyes. "Please."

She gripped his throat. Not hard enough to choke him. Not hard enough to block his airway, but a nice heavy weight that he was sure to feel.

"Okay?" she asked. He swallowed hard, and she felt it on her palm.

"Yes. *Yes.*" His free hand left her thigh and fisted the sheet.

"I'm gonna come," she told him. It was sneaking up on her slowly—that fluttering in her core, the sweet achy pleasure.

He stared up at her as she fell apart, and she stared down at him until ecstasy slammed her eyes shut. She couldn't hold herself up, and she crashed into his arms.

He caught her.

It took a few seconds for her to realize that Leo had pulled her off his cock and ditched the vibrator. He was breathing very deliberately, in through his nose out through his mouth.

"Are you all right?" she asked, her voice rough.

"Yup. Just … that was super hot, and I feel like I'm on fire … and I want to come so badly."

She laughed and kissed him. She had expected him to orgasm when she did, but she was happy he hadn't. He opened to her kiss, and she claimed it.

When she pulled back, nerves started to get the better of her. She tried to cover it by being as matter-of-fact as possible. She stripped his condom off and carefully removed his plug. He was shivery. Goosebumps bloomed over his arms and legs.

"Any trick to putting this on?" she asked, holding up the harness and a purple silicone dildo. The harness looked like a jock with adjustable straps.

Summer of Rosie: pegging master.

"Not really." He helped her fasten the dildo to the harness, and before she knew it, she was wearing the whole contraption. It felt strange and powerful and sexy. "How do you want me?" he asked. "Please say fast."

She wanted to go slow because of that comment, but he deserved his reward. He shoved a pillow under his hips. She lubed up the dildo and notched the head to his hole. He held his own legs back.

"Ready?"

"Yes, Rosie. Fuck me."

She pressed in slowly. A moan punched out of his chest. Once she was fully seated inside him, she stilled.

All his emotions were on the surface. He seemed so vulnerable and open.

"Leo." The words *I love you* jumped to her throat, but

she bottled them up. Instead, she moved, fucking him, and said his name, again and again. "Leo. Leo. Leo."

---

LEO WAS bad at staying quiet while he was being fucked. It dragged every noise from his throat. Each time Rosie pushed into him, he cried out or groaned or grunted. He couldn't help it.

It wasn't going to take him long. His body was on high alert from being teased to the edge of reason. His prostate was extra sensitive after having the plug bumping up against it for so long, and his cock ached from holding back his orgasm.

That wasn't what was overwhelming him, though. The sensations in his body were taking a backseat to the broken way Rosie was saying his name.

He loved his name on her lips. He loved the way she planted a hand on his ribcage, her fingers pressing into his skin. He loved the shine in her eyes. He loved her.

Fuck.

They were too good together.

Too good together to just give this up.

"Rosie," he gasped as she picked up speed. She was amazing at this. Better than he could have ever expected. He put his hand over hers on his ribs, tangling their fingers together.

That felt more intimate than everything else they'd done. They were holding hands.

"What do you need, baby?" she asked. "Tell me what to do."

"A hand. I need to touch my cock."

"I'll do it."

She put her weight on his ribs, boxing him in. Then she spit into her other hand, which was so dirty he almost popped without anything on his cock at all.

He clenched down as she put her slick hand on his prick, and she slowed her thrusting, making each one count as she massaged his crown. She'd remembered. Focused attention on his tip was exactly how he liked it. She'd remembered and something about that was so beautiful and so heartbreaking.

"Oh God," he breathed. "Rosie, I love"—heat flushed through him—"*this*. I love this. Fuck, yes. Please."

His body locked tight. Sparks burst behind his eyelids, bright blooming eruptions of color. He bucked on the cock inside him and came in a rush over Rosie's hand and his stomach.

The orgasm rocked him. He couldn't talk, and his vision fuzzed out.

By the time he was able to have any semblance of a conversation, Rosie had already taken off the strap-on and cleaned up his stomach with a washrag.

"Hi," he said. His voice was shaky.

"Hi. Are you okay?"

He nodded. "That was incredible."

"Yeah?"

"Yes. Rosie. Fuck." Little ripples of pleasure were still hitting him. He felt wrung out.

She crawled into bed with him and maneuvered them under the covers. She looked like an angel—naked, her hair a halo on his pillow, skin golden from his reading lamp.

A rowdy determination filled him. He'd always gone against the grain to some degree. He enjoyed rebelling. There was absolutely no fucking reason his relationship with Rosie needed to be any different. She expected it to go one particular way. He would do his damnedest to prove her wrong.

"I'm going to the farmer's market tomorrow with my mom," he said. "Will you come with me?"

Rosie tensed. "Your mom?"

"Yeah, she loves shopping. I'd love it if you would join us."

He watched Rosie's face closely. When they'd been eighteen, Rosie had worked for his parents at Froth and Forage. She'd been a hostess. He'd reluctantly been a waiter. Rosie's grandma had been a prep cook—one of the three jobs she'd had to keep their family afloat.

He and Rosie had kept their relationship a secret because there was too much at stake, mainly her grandma's position. His mom and dad would not have been happy about him dating Rosie, not only because she was one of their employees but also because she wasn't part of their country club set. But, Leo had to admit, the main reason he and Rosie had snuck around was because he'd enjoyed pulling one over on his family. It had fueled that defiant flame inside him.

Things were different now, though. Running away

seemed to have cured his parents of a lot of their expectations for him. They accepted him. They wanted him to be happy. Sometimes, he was pretty sure they were even proud of him.

He wanted it to be different with Rosie too.

"That seems ... strange to me," she said.

"How so?" he asked.

She huffed. "Are you in the habit of introducing your fuck buddies to your mom, Leo?"

He started to say that she was more than a fuck buddy but decided that was the wrong tack. She *was* more than a fuck buddy. He was going to figure out a way to make this work between them without either one compromising pieces of themselves. He could do it, but he needed to play his cards a bit closer to his chest when it came to Rosie Holiday. She would bolt. He saw the fear in her eyes.

"They've met Dean. I think we can leave the *fuck* part out of the explanation, don't you?"

Her expression was mutinous. "I suppose."

"It'll be fun. I promise."

"I'm trusting you."

"I swear, Rosie, that's all I've ever wanted. Other than spending the night together. I want that too."

They'd never gotten that as teenagers. It wasn't exactly easy to have sleepovers when you were stuck under your parents' or grandmother's roof. He wanted to revel in it. In having her against him. In the warmth as their bodies pressed together. In their eventual morning breath.

She smiled and tucked her head under his chin. "The week after Landon moved out, Sasha came and slept with me. I was in shock, I think. I was glad he'd moved out. I didn't want to be around him, but I also kept searching for him in my sleep. It was hard."

He couldn't imagine what that had been like. He'd never had a constant in his life. With Mal, their time together had been so disjointed that they hadn't really had routines. "I'm so sorry you went through that."

She snuggled closer. "It sucked, but I learned a lot about myself. I don't want to rely on anyone else for my happiness. I don't want my identity to be wrapped up in other people. I want to be Rosie, not Landon's wife. Or anyone's fucking wife. I don't need a perpetual bed partner, you know? Cuddling is nice. Sleeping with you will be fantastic. I won't take it for granted, but it's also not the core of what I need long term."

Leo's heart thumped. "What do you need long term?"

A beat of silence passed between them. Finally, she said, "Security. Independence ... Respect."

He could give her all those things.

"Love?" he asked.

"No." Her voice was starting to fade with sleep. "Love hasn't ever given me anything but pain."

## Chapter Ten

O ne of the best things about summer for Rosie was not having to wake up at the butt crack of dawn. Thus, she was distinctly unhappy to find herself in the parking lot of a skating rink at seven in the morning, but Leo had bribed her with the possibility of food samples, so she'd rolled out of his bed, showered, brushed her teeth, and donned a baseball cap to cover her wet hair.

Leo grabbed her hand as they walked through the parking lot to the front of the farmers market. Her heart jumped into her throat. The morning sun was pleasant and golden. The scent of produce and flowers was in the air. Leo was holding her hand.

It felt like a date from a rom-com, but it shouldn't have felt like a date at all! They weren't dating.

She kind of wanted to have a big long pout about the fact that he was making this feel so nice. She didn't have time to pout, though. She had to gird her loins for encountering Mirabella Shawcross-Whittaker, who was frankly the most terrifying woman Rosie had ever met and also possibly the most badass.

"Leo, darling," said a posh voice from behind them.

Rosie flinched. She'd meant to drop Leo's hand before they saw his mother. She hadn't expected the woman to sneak up on them.

They let go of each other and turned around. Leo gave his mom a kiss on the cheek. Mirabella had changed a lot in the last thirteen years. Granted, Rosie had only ever seen Mirabella when she was in boss mode at Froth and Forage.

Today, though, Leo's mother seemed carefree and relaxed. She was wearing a tennis dress, dazzling white sneakers, and a visor. She had one of those ageless faces, probably via Botox—which, like, good for her, she looked amazing—and feathery white-blonde hair.

"Well, what do we have here, Leo?" Mirabella asked.

"Mom, this is Rosie Holiday. She used to work at the restaurant. Do you remember her?"

Mirabella smiled gently—an expression Rosie had never seen from her—and said, "Of course I do. Your grandmother was the only prep cook I trusted."

That was the perfect thing to say to put Rosie at ease. She'd loved her grandma, and anyone who recognized how special that woman had been was fine in Rosie's book.

"Nice to see you again, Mrs. Shawcross-Whittaker," Rosie said, shaking her hand.

"Oh, goodness. Call me Mira." *Yeah, that was never gonna happen.* "But you didn't answer my question, son."

Mirabella turned to Leo. "Did I spy a bit of hand holding?"

Rosie flushed. She should never have let Leo take her hand.

"Mom, don't embarrass me." Leo sounded so much like his surly teenaged self that Rosie almost laughed.

Almost. But she didn't because she was too freaked out.

Mirabella turned her formidable gaze on Rosie. "You do know he draws porn for a living, right?"

"I don't make porn!" Leo said, causing the man selling cabbage nearby to glance at them in surprise.

"Excuse me, darling. You do know that he draws himself having sex for a living, right? It's very good stuff I've heard. I can't bring myself to look at it too closely." Mirabella flipped her hair over her shoulder and stared placidly at Rosie.

"I know what he does for a living, yes."

"And what do you do?"

"I'm a kindergarten teacher."

A heavy pause followed Rosie's words before Mirabella laughed so hard she snorted. "Oh, that's rich. A kindergarten teacher and an erotic artist. I love it. Come here, lovely. Tell me more about yourself."

Mirabella took Rosie's hand and tucked it in her elbow, leading Rosie through booth after booth and asking questions about her job, siblings, marital history, and home.

"Mom, you can stop with the third degree," Leo said, tagging along behind them.

"No, I cannot." She gently squeezed Rosie's arm. "I've never seen Leo hold anyone's hand. I saw him kiss that Dean boy once in the restaurant's parking lot, but holding hands is different."

Rosie thought it might be different too, which was why this whole thing terrified her.

"We're friends," Rosie said, her voice stilted. "That's all."

"Hmm. Okay." Mirabella seemed to see through her. "You must come to our Fourth of July dinner party. It'll be divine."

Leo jumped in. "We have plans."

*Thank God.* Rosie thought a dinner party at chez Whittaker sounded about as fun as getting her teeth pulled.

"Are you lying to me?" Mirabella asked her son.

"No. We're going to a barbecue at our friend Robin's house."

That was news to Rosie. Exciting news. She knew what happened at Lady Robin's.

Orgies. Orgies happened there.

"Well, fine. If you don't want to spend time with your family, then so be it," Mirabella sniped. Leo winked at Rosie behind his mom's back as she continued, "Let's shop. Have you ever made jam, Rosie?"

"No. I'm not really a cook."

"Oh, pish. Making jam isn't cooking. It's boiling. Here." Mirabella handed a huge reusable shopping bag to Leo. "You two can make jam together. It'll be ... cute. We'll get you everything you need to make something yummy."

The grin that stretched Leo's face made Rosie think she'd fallen into a trap. She didn't know how to prevent this steamrolling. She didn't know if she wanted to prevent it.

"It'll have to be at your house, Rosie," Leo said. "Do you mind?"

"Umm, I guess not?"

Before Rosie could blink, Mirabella had dumped a bushel of dill, five heads of garlic, and three onions into the bag.

"This is for the jam?" Rosie asked, then immediately felt ridiculous.

"No. You're making pickles too," Mirabella said.

"*I* am?"

"Yes. Do you like dill pickles?"

"I do. I guess."

"Great. This is Leo's favorite treat."

"Mom," Leo said, his voice full of warning. Not much good it was going to do. His mother was determined to make Rosie a canner, it seemed.

"It'll be fun!" his mother said, a winning smile on her face. "Cucumbers. Ah. Here we are. Hello, Mr. Woolenbury."

As Mirabella chatted with the cucumber farmer, Leo drew Rosie into his arms, his hand on the back of her neck.

He kissed her temple. "I'm sorry."

"I think your mom's my hero," Rosie said, and he laughed.

She let him hold her. This was a date. A date with his

mother in attendance, but still. Everything was colorful and warm and artificially pastoral. She loved it.

Mirabella returned with an obscene amount of cucumbers. "Now, the jam. You'll have to buy pectin and jars of course. Leo will tell you what you need." She threw a huge ginger root in the bag and a handful of lemons.

Rosie and Leo followed along behind Mirabella as she chattered away. Every once in a while, she'd scold Leo for some silly thing. Rosie got the feeling both mother and son enjoyed that, like it was a game between them.

Leo held Rosie's hand as they perused tables of local honey and studied pots of sunflowers taller than them. He led her through booths full of peaches and apples and carrots of every conceivable color. They taste-tested salsas and sauerkrauts and olive oils. They bought fresh-squeezed grapefruit juice and breakfast empanadas. Rosie let it all happen in a pleasurable daze.

Then, after Mirabella divvied up their farmers market haul, she hugged Rosie, enveloping her in a cloud of Chanel No. 5. "I'm so glad you were here today, Rosie," she said simply. "You make him smile."

Their perfect morning cracked into a million pieces because Leo made Rosie smile too, and it wasn't fair. Leo wasn't going to be around for regular farmers market dates. Rosie wasn't going to get to spend weird mornings with the indomitable Mirabella Shawcross-Whittaker. That wasn't what this was supposed to be.

Working through a checklist of sexcapades was very

different than going on the best date of her entire life, and it was all Leo's fault.

---

BY MIDMORNING, Rosie was neck deep in vinegar and cucumbers. Her entire kitchen counter was covered in the prettiest peaches she'd ever seen, and Leo kissed her neck or touched her butt every time he squeezed past her.

"I just put this big ass jar on my porch, and the sun does all the work?" Rosie asked. She loved the way the cucumbers, dill, garlic, and onions layered in the glass jar. It was pretty.

"Yep. They're sun pickles. It'll take at least three days. Maybe longer if it's cloudy."

She felt a small prick of unhappiness. Leo would be leaving in three days. He wouldn't even get to enjoy these stupid sun pickles.

She followed him into her backyard and watched as he placed the jar on an exposed bit of patio.

"This is a nice space," he said, looking around.

She thought so too. It was one of the reasons she'd bought this condo. There was a privacy fence separating her from her neighbors, a pretty patio, and a big shade tree in the corner.

"I wish I could enhance the backyard," she said. "Make it more usable and homey." She wasn't particularly handy, but she had dreams of a porch swing and flowerbeds and bird feeders.

"I could help you with that."

She glared at him, and he grinned. He couldn't help her with that, and he fucking knew it. She stomped back inside.

"So what's up with these peaches?" she asked. They'd bought a million of them. They were dainty and fresh and fuzzy.

"These peaches and this ginger"—he held up the large root—"are going to be the base for the best jam you've ever had."

"You talk a big jam game," she said. "I'm not convinced you'll be able to deliver."

"And what will you give me if I do?" He snuggled up behind her and smelled her hair. She'd noticed he did that a lot.

She closed her eyes. "Jam?"

He laughed. "Fair enough."

She sighed and glanced around at the mess in her kitchen. There were canning contraptions everywhere. It was very intimidating.

"We'll start with boiling the jars," Leo said.

From there they scored the peaches and set up an assembly line of blanching—boiling the peaches for a few seconds, then dunking them in an ice bath. The scent of peaches filled her kitchen, and buttery sunrays filtered in through her windows.

"This is one of my favorite things to do in the summer, but it's hard in my Airstream. Not enough room." Leo transferred another round of peaches from the boiling water to the ice water. "Thank you for letting me commandeer your day."

That made her feel guilty for all her unhappy thoughts. She wasn't truly unhappy. She was super happy, in fact, which was the problem. She was enjoying this way too much.

"You're welcome. It's fun," she grumbled.

"You ready to peel?"

"I guess."

She picked a peach out of the ice bath. It was soft and slightly warm. She had no idea how she was supposed to peel it, but she figured the *x* they'd scored on the bottom would be a good place to start.

She made a right mess while trying to get the skin off. She managed to squish about half the peach in the process. When she'd finished, she plucked the stone out and turned to Leo in triumph. His eyes were full of heat and humor.

She grabbed another with a smile, loving the way he was staring at her. She'd made it through two peaches before Leo wrapped his arms around her from behind.

"I could show you how to do it quicker. My way is also less messy."

She liked the mess, but she didn't tell him that. Instead, she said, "You want to pool stick me."

"What?"

"Yeah, oldest move in the book. The man puts his arms around the lady to show her how to shoot pool. But with peaches."

He laughed and kissed the back of her neck. Goosebumps bloomed over her shoulders, and she dropped her peach on the counter.

"Watching you do that is turning me on," he whispered in her ear. "Watching you do anything would turn me on, but this is really getting to me."

She huffed and picked her peach back up. She squeezed the flesh out of the skin. He made a sexy rumbly noise in the back of his throat.

"Oh my god, you perv," she said with a laugh.

"I know. I'm sorry." He mouthed along her shoulder.

"If you'd get your own hands dirty, this would go faster."

"Okay." He placed one last gentle kiss on the space between her shoulder blades, which were exposed because she was wearing a tank top.

That was *her spot*. It was guaranteed to make her wet. Hot tingles zipped along her spine, and she felt her pulse in her throat. She turned in his arms. His eyes were full of fire, and for once, he didn't wait for her to kiss him or to order him around.

He licked into her mouth like he was trying to get to the center of her. Like he was reaching for the pit, digging it out with his tongue. She moaned, stunned by the viscous desire flowing through her.

Her palms were sticky and covered in peach, so she tried not to touch anything, holding her hands out to the sides. He brought her hand to his lips, then he sucked her thumb into his mouth, his tongue twining around it, and swallowed.

A high, shocked noise left her throat. She painted a

stripe of juicy rosy-orange fruit across his bottom lip before following the path with her mouth. Their kiss tasted of summer.

"This is not sanitary," she said breathlessly.

"Live a little, sweetheart. We'll wash our hands."

---

THEIR TWENTY-MINUTE INTERLUDE resulted in an astounding blowjob—in the living room because Rosie was fastidious about food safety—and Leo needing a shower to wash off the juice from Rosie's sticky hands. Leo couldn't help but notice that giving him head had *not* been on Rosie's summer sex checklist. She'd stepped outside her plans, which he found heartening. Maybe she would be able to see the possibilities for them, that they could be more than a fun experiment.

Now, Rosie was arranging all the jars of peach and ginger jam on her counter. She had this bright-eyed look about her.

"What are you thinking, Rosie Posey?" he asked.

She smiled—a big, uninhibited one that about took his breath away. He was gone over this woman.

"I have a label maker. I could create adorable labels for this adorable jam and give it to everyone I love." She put her hand over her mouth. "I sound like a mommy blogger."

He laughed and pulled her into his arms. "Do I get any of this love jam?"

She wrinkled her nose. "Gross."

"Come on, let's eat some." He grabbed the one jar where the seal hadn't taken on the lid—meaning they needed to eat it immediately—and a loaf of raisin bread he'd bought at the farmers market. Then he headed for the backdoor.

"Where are you going?"

"To sit outside. Grab a picnic blanket, please?"

She eyed him suspiciously but retrieved a handful of silverware and a blanket from her living room. He helped her lay it out in the shade of the big tree in her backyard.

It was hot outside, but the shade made it bearable. They heard kids lighting firecrackers in the street. Loud reports and pops followed by giggles. It was the best summer picnic soundtrack. Leo sliced them bread and slathered it with fresh peach jam. Rosie made herself comfortable with her head on his thigh and hummed as she took her first bite.

"This is perfect," she said, her eyes closed. She was wearing a baseball cap—she'd turned it backwards during the makeout and blowjob—but he wanted to play with her hair, so he removed it.

"It is." He ran his fingers through her tangled strands.

She opened her eyes. "I loved making the jam," she said slowly.

"Good."

"No, you don't get it."

He took a bite, enjoying the sweetness of the peach, the citrus burst from the lemon zest, and the zing of ginger. "Tell me then."

"I want to make more. Oh my." She sat up. "I was just lying here thinking about how I could make jam for people for their birthdays and Christmas and potlucks and parties, and all the different recipes I could try. I could make tomato jam or blueberry vanilla or jalapeno strawberry. I could be the jam lady."

"Okay." She was obviously having some sort of epiphany, but he wasn't quite following it.

"I want to be the jam lady. Leo!" She gave him a smacking kiss on the lips. "That was the most fun I've had in ages—sex with you notwithstanding, of course."

"To be fair, the jam making included sex."

She waved that away. "That's because you sexualized the peaches."

A shocked laugh slipped out of his throat. Before he could refute that, she straddled his lap. Her hair flew around her face. She slapped her hat back onto her head, turning it backwards again.

"Thank you," she said. "Thank you for teaching me. Seeing my little creations lined up in my kitchen, I haven't felt that way since—" She shook her head.

He was walloped by the desire to paint her like this. Backwards hat, peach stain on her tank top, dappled by sunlight through the leaves of the tree. She was the most beautiful creature he'd ever held in his hands. It was so overwhelming, his feelings for her. His heart was beating a weird tattoo in his chest. His stomach hurt. His palms ached.

She needed to know. They needed to talk about this.

Come up with a plan. A plan that wasn't, "Hey, let's fuck when you drive through town."

He loved her. Still.

"Rosie, I think I l—"

She frowned, panic flitting through her eyes, and stopped his words with a kiss. "No. Not yet," she murmured against his lips.

Surprise and pain washed through him, but he nodded. She stuffed another bite of jam and bread into his mouth as if he didn't get the picture.

He got the picture. She wasn't ready for that conversation yet.

She'd found a hobby that made her happy. She could be a jam-making fiend. She could stop feeling like that blank slate.

And she absolutely did not want Leo to kill her vibe with talk of love and the future. That message came through loud and clear.

## Chapter Eleven

The window at the Lady Robin's Independence Day Pop-up Party had a display of red and blue lingerie on glossy, white, faceless mannequins. The mannequins were holding peaches and American flags, except for one that was holding an eggplant.

Rosie laughed as she studied the display. It was clever, sexy, and trendy. She spotted her brother and his boyfriend crossing the street to reach the temporary Lady Robin's storefront. She and Benji used to try to plan their trips to these pop-up shops so they wouldn't be there at the same time. Rosie had figured there was nothing quite as awkward as seeing your older sister purchase dildos from your other older sister, but, eventually, it became too much trouble to arrange. Benji wasn't shy about sex, so there was no reason Rosie should be either.

Benji sidled up to her, slinging his arm over her shoulder. "I'm here to meet your boy toy."

"What?" She didn't like the sound of that. Leo was in

there selling his art. She'd forgotten that Sasha had let that slip in their group text.

"I can't wait."

William mouthed, "I'm sorry," to her, and she sighed.

"That's a new Wren Rebello piece," Benji said, pointing to a mannequin wearing a blue jock with gold straps. "She gave me an early promo for my Instagram."

"That's cool." Rosie followed Benji's lingerie influencer Instagram account, but she rarely opened the app. It wasn't exactly fun seeing the exciting stuff everyone was doing when she was sitting at home being boring. Though, she had posted a picture of her cute jars of jam yesterday. It was proof (to herself, at least) that the Summer of Rosie had been somewhat successful.

Maybe she could be a jam influencer. A jam influencer by day and a pegging queen by night. She had hobbies now.

"Let's go inside. Babe, do you have our shopping list?" Benji asked William.

William held up an actual itemized list. It was long. Benji pulled Rosie into the shop.

Rosie went to all the Lady Robin's Intimate Implement pop-up shops, but none of them had ever been like this one. It kind of felt like patriotism had thrown up in the space, but there were also sex toys everywhere. It was fabulous and irreverent and so perfectly Lady Robin's.

Leo was at a busy table toward the back of the shop, surrounded by shoppers. She would say hello to him soon. In the meantime, Benji skipped off with William to look at a display of Fleshjacks, and Rosie found Sasha, who was manning a table of Lady Robin's newest small-batch dildos.

Rosie gave her sister a hug. "This is amazing, Sasha. You guys outdid yourselves."

"Thank you. Robin let me name these after fireworks." Sasha gestured over the display of silicone toys in front of her. She started at one end and tapped each dildo, telling Rosie the name. "Saturn Missile, Bombette, Chrysanthemum, and Silver Salute."

"They're pretty." They were all covered in different glittery patterns with a dark base color, like a galaxy, or, Rosie supposed, like fireworks. She picked up the Bombette. It was short and fat with a wicked curved head. The design on it was dark navy blue with shiny red sparkles. "I want this one."

Sasha grinned and handed her a boxed Bombette. Rosie heard Leo's laugh, gruff and warm, from the other side of the room. She turned to see him having a conversation with Benji.

"That's a disaster waiting to happen," Rosie said under her breath. Another customer needed Sasha, so Rosie moved toward the outer wall to get a better view of Leo's art displayed around the room. She recognized some of it from *Characters*, but seeing the originals was very different than viewing the prints in the book.

There were superheroes and soldiers and one very sexy Statue of Liberty. Her favorite, though, was a Black woman posed like Rosie the Riveter. The woman's jumpsuit was open to her belly button and a slip of nipple was visible. She had tattoos on her arms and a trans flag pin on her lapel.

"That one's gorgeous, huh?"

Rosie turned toward the voice to find Robin Erco watching her from behind a lemonade station.

"He's talented," Rosie said. The novelty straws in the lemonade had little strippers hanging off them. Rosie picked up a glass.

"He is that."

Rosie tried to hide her smile. She knew just how talented Leo was, in all the ways.

"Whitt told me you guys were coming to my barbecue."

It took a second for Rosie to remember that Leo's friends called him Whitt.

"I hope you don't mind me crashing," Rosie said.

"Of course not! It's been too long since we've hung out."

"It has. I'm sorry."

Robin was part of a huge friend group that included Sasha, William, and Wren Rebello. Way back when, before Rosie's marriage had fallen apart, she had been part of that crowd. It was impossible to explain the ways Landon had incrementally pulled her away from them.

"No big deal. The best friendships are the ones that can withstand a bit of space, time, and weirdness."

"Thank you. I agree."

"So, the barbecue. You know what will probably happen if you stay late enough, correct?" Robin sounded very much like the badass businesswoman she was.

Rosie blushed. "I'm aware."

"And you're okay with that?"

"Yes."

"Wonderful. I'm sure there will be no shortage of people who would be happy to help you put Leo in his place. Present company included. Not that you need help. I suspect you're quite adept."

Rosie's mouth went dry as she met Robin's eyes. It shouldn't have come as a surprise that Leo's desires were so well known, and Robin was a beautiful woman. The thought of *Lady Robin* being involved in whatever happened between her and Leo was not unappealing. In fact, it was the opposite.

They chatted for a few more minutes. Rosie told her about the jam she'd made, promising to bring some to the party. They spoke about Benji's new kite obsession, and the flawlessness of Sasha's small wedding the month previous.

Then Robin said, "I was pretty thrilled to be able to get Whitt here on the day his book released."

Rosie blinked a few times. She hadn't been aware it was his release day.

An employee with a question caught Robin's attention, so Rosie approached Leo. When she got close enough, he stood up and gave her a kiss over the table. It simultaneously embarrassed her and thrilled her to be claimed in front of, well, her entire family.

"Hey you," Leo said, his voice sending a sexy twist to her stomach.

"Hi. I saw you met my brother. He's a handful."

"He gave me the shotgun speech."

She frowned. "What's the shotgun speech?"

"The whole 'don't hurt my sister' spiel. I've gotten one from both your siblings. They love you."

"Oh. That little punk, I swear to God."

Leo laughed and grabbed her hand. "It was funny. He was very sweet about it. I told him his boyfriend was hot and gushing about his silver fox distracted him. Then he asked me about my Airstream. He wants to come see it."

"He does classic-car restoration. Not surprised he'd be into the idea of your RV."

"I told him not to worry," Leo said.

"About the Airstream?"

"No. About me hurting you. I have no intention of doing that, Rosie."

Leo's intentions had nothing to do with it. He might not plan on tearing her apart, but that didn't mean it wouldn't happen. He'd started to bring it up yesterday, when they'd been out in her backyard. She could tell he'd wanted to talk about *them*. She hadn't been ready to face the music in that regard. She still wasn't ready.

"Congratulations on your book. You didn't tell me today was special." She tapped the cover of *Lovers*.

Pink spots dotted his cheeks. "I don't like to make a big deal out of it. I was lucky enough to have a gallery show, so it seems silly to celebrate twice."

"Shut up. This is cool," she said sternly. She picked up a copy. "Will you sign this for me?"

He peered up at her, his bottom lip caught between

his teeth. "No. Not yet," he said, echoing her words from the day before. "I will before I leave."

So much for locking down her emotions when it came to Leo Whittaker. She gave him another kiss, bought a bag of sex toys to make herself feel better, and left.

---

THE MORNING of the Fourth of July was sweltering. Leo had stepped out of his Airstream to drink his coffee outside and had promptly turned back around to seek air conditioning.

Rosie was asleep in his bed. She had spent the night again. He'd fucked her with the prettiest dildo he'd ever seen before she'd ordered him to jerk off. It had been amazing and easy. Comfortable but also hot. He imagined a million mornings together. A million summer days in his Airstream, traveling all over. A million fall, winter, and spring nights in her condo. He had an awesome plan, if only Rosie would let him voice it.

He walked over to his canvas. He'd been messing with it over the last few days, and an image had started to take shape yesterday morning before the pop-up party. It felt like a yearlong seed come to fruition. The origin story of *Lovers*, finally on canvas. It was different than his other paintings. Evocative rather than bluntly erotic. Not a piece he'd ever try to sell, which was fine by him because it was a tad more personal than he was used to, and that was saying something, considering the subject matter of his other work.

He painted for another hour, lost in that space he fell into while working. It was the same feeling he got sometimes during sex—peace mixed with excitement. The calm and the storm.

When he eventually blinked himself out of his concentration and took in the painting, he realized it was almost done. An unusual pain spread through him.

Perspective—that was what he needed, and he knew exactly how to get it. He washed his hands and retrieved his phone from the bedroom. He needed to make a call. It was early—Rosie didn't stir—but the person he wanted to talk to would be awake.

He stepped out into the oppressive heat and sat down at the picnic table at the back of his campsite. It was in the shade.

The phone rang a few times before a soft voice answered, "Hello?"

"Hey, Mal. Happy Fourth of July." Leo normally called Mal this week, knowing he struggled with it.

That earned Leo a disgruntled scoff. "Yeah, yeah. I hate today."

"I know. Did you and Tommy go to the cabin this week?" Leo asked.

"Yeah. We were able to get away from the noise, which was nice."

"I'm glad." It was a relief that Mal was away from the commotion of fireworks and firecrackers. Leo had always enjoyed Independence Day, not because he was particularly patriotic, but because he liked the excitement of parades and parties. He loved this culmination of summertime and the crackle of adrenaline during a fireworks show. It wasn't until he'd met Mal that he'd realized how difficult this week was for some people.

"Where are you?" Mal asked.

"A picnic table outside the Airstream."

"That's not what I meant." Mal laughed, and Leo's discomfort eased. It was an old joke between them. Mal would ask where Leo was, wanting the name of the town, but Leo would over-localize his answer. He'd say he was in a bar with peanut shells on the floors or a park with no slide. "How are you, really?"

The leaves above Leo rustled as two bluebirds seemed to fight for territory. He leaned back and watched the show. "I've made a mess of a sticky situation, so about the same as usual."

Even though he and Mal weren't together, they were there for each other. He trusted Mal's opinion.

"What happened?"

"Ran into an old love, and I—"

"An old love?" Mal said, delight in his voice. Leo closed his eyes. "As far as I know, the only loves you've ever had are me—thank you—and that girl from your hometown."

"Ding, ding, ding."

"What's her name again?"

"Rosie."

"Ah yes. Rosie. So sweet. You ran into Rosie and *what*?"

"And I still love her, Mal. She's wonderful, and it feels right. This relationship is worth fighting for."

They both let the words hang there, the unspoken bits spreading out between them like spilled paint. They'd broken up because Leo hadn't been willing to fight for them, among a million other reasons.

"What's the problem, then?" Mal asked.

Leo sighed. "I'm scared."

"Oh, hon."

Tears pricked the back of Leo's eyes. When Mal used that tone on him, it hit him in the breadbasket.

"I don't feel pulled in a million different directions with her. The world's not clawing at me so hard. I'm clear-headed and inspired. I think I might like to slow down if I got to slow down with her." A beat of silence followed his words. "What?"

Mal hummed. "I hope you're not saying you're ready to plant your flag somewhere permanently. I love you, Whitt, but that isn't you. The impulse to run would eventually rip you apart. You need a partner who can run with you."

"No, see, I have this plan. A compromise. I could—"

"Now you want to compromise?" Mal said, his voice incredulous. Memories of a hundred small spats rushed to the surface. "Ignore me."

"No. I'm sorry. I didn't mean to hurt you."

"I know." Mal sounded world-weary and exhausted. "I'm not the only one who got hurt. Your heart was broken. My heart was broken. It sucked, but I wasn't alone at the end, and you were. I'll regret that until the day I die. Love isn't supposed to burn hot like a fire-cracker and explode in your face. We loved each other, but it wasn't enough. We got burned. I don't want you to get burned again, but I also hate for you to be alone."

Leo rubbed a hand over the back of his neck. He was sweating. "I don't want my needs to hurt anyone else. I can't stand still for too long. Can't stay in one place without feeling caged. Rosie needs security and stability. That was why we broke up initially, but we're older."

"You are. How long has it been? Twelve, thirteen years?"

"Yeah."

"The difference a decade and some change can make," Mal said.

Career changes and marriages and relationships and death. So much had happened.

"I believe ... I have to believe that Rosie and I finding each other again is a sign. I've been painting her in my head for thirteen years, Mal. Maybe all my searching has been to find a way back to her, and frankly, I don't think we need to be in each other's pockets constantly for our relationship to work. I think it might be better if we're not, even." He thought back to Rosie saying she wanted security, independence, and respect. She wanted those things of her own volition.

Now that he was speaking his longing out loud, he felt hope take wing in his chest. This could work.

The door of the Airstream opened and Rosie popped her head out. She had showered. Her hair was wet, and Leo spied a bare shoulder.

"Mal, I gotta go. Rosie just woke up."

"Send me a picture of her," Mal said. "I need to lay eyes on the person who has finally brought you to your knees. Emotionally. Not sexually. We all know you like that."

Leo laughed. "Talk to you soon."

"You too. Oh, and Leo?"

"Uh-huh?"

"I'm happy for you. You deserve love, but don't give up the essence of yourself in order to have it. That's not love. It's a shadow of it. Okay?"

"Okay." Leo hung up and smiled at Rosie. His mind was reeling. "Go put clothes on, then come enjoy the morning with me."

She narrowed her eyes. "Don't order me around, Leo Whittaker."

"Oh, I wouldn't dare."

She smiled and closed the door, but returned not three minutes later. She was wearing one of his T-shirts and a pair of running shorts. Her hair was drying into frizzy waves. He wanted more mornings with her. More mornings to see Rosie before she donned that straight-laced mask she showed the rest of the world.

"What's up?" she asked. They rearranged themselves until she was sitting on the picnic table and he was standing between her legs.

"I leave tomorrow."

She tensed. "I'm aware."

"No need to sound so suspicious," he said with a

laugh. She scrunched up her nose and glanced away from him. "Hey, I'm serious. We're going to be okay."

"I don't want to talk about this," she admitted. "It's easier to pretend it's not happening."

"It is, though. I think we should be able to have a conversation about it, don't you?"

"Speak for yourself," she mumbled under her breath. He couldn't keep in his chuckle. He loved her grumpiness. He just really fucking loved her.

"We don't have to talk yet, but it's coming soon."

She nodded. "Tomorrow. Before you leave."

"Tomorrow," he said.

She hopped off the table, and he saw the panic in her eyes.

"Can I have a kiss before you run out of here like I've set you on fire?"

She stalked back over and grabbed a hank of his hair. He melted under her hands, under her lips. This was too good to give up without a fight.

She pushed him away and groaned. "Ugh. You're distracting."

He smiled. "I'll see you tonight. Remember, we have an orgy to attend."

"As if I could forget."

## Chapter Twelve

The Fourth of July barbecue was rocking. There was delicious food everywhere and leftover decorations from the Lady Robin's Independence Day Pop-up Party. A group of men were planning out where to shoot off fireworks, excited like a bunch of teenagers, ready to blow shit up. A few people were playing in the pool. And Rosie was beating her sister and brother-in-law, Perry, at cornhole.

Rosie's cornhole partner, Wren Rebello, made her toss. It knocked one of Perry's beanbags off the board. Wren threw her hands in the air and yelled, "Eat shit, Perry."

Rosie laughed, slightly horrified. She'd forgotten how competitive Wren could be.

"She's cutthroat," Rosie whispered to Sasha.

"It's the roller derby. Brings out the best in her. She and Robin both do it."

"When did that start?"

"A few months ago." Sasha turned to Rosie abruptly. "Oh my god, you'd be so good at that."

"At what?"

"At roller derby! Wren, Rosie wants to join your roller derby team!"

"Excuse me?" Rosie said.

Wren dropped her bag and rushed over. "That would be amazing. We suck, but it's so fun." She grabbed Rosie's hand and tugged her away from the game.

"Hey, we were winning."

Wren waved that off. "We'll come up with an awesome derby name for you. You need to get out all that repressed aggression. This will be great. Robin!"

Robin was holding court on her large back patio. Her house was beautiful, a true testament to her hard work and empire. It was modern and extravagant, built on the bluff edge above the river.

Today, Robin was wearing a black leather bustier top and a red tulip skirt. Her hair was down and wild with waves. She looked like a supermodel, beautiful and unapproachable.

Wren had no such qualms. She wiggled down next to Robin on the lounge chair and pulled Rosie directly in front of them.

"Rosie wants to join the Slammin' Sirens," Wren said.

Robin reached out and delicately caught Rosie's index finger with her own. "Does she really?"

A weird mix of emotions swirled through Rosie, most too convoluted to understand, but one stood out. Excitement.

"I don't know," she said. It was safer to hold things close.

"It would be fun," Robin said.

Rosie didn't doubt that. She had missed Robin and Wren. They were more Sasha's friends than hers, and now Benji was folded into that group via his connection to William. It would be nice to have something that was hers. A way to connect with these people who had always been there for her.

"What are your derby names?" Rosie asked.

"Oh, I'm Stitch Bitch and Robin is Madame Ballcrusher," Wren said.

A laugh choked Rosie. Those names were perfect.

"I'll think about it," Rosie said.

She felt someone at her back. Then strong arms. Leo kissed the side of her neck.

"What are you talking about?" he asked. He smelled like flash powder from the firecrackers he'd been shooting off. It made her a little dizzy.

"Roller derby," Wren said. "Rosie's going to join our team. Can't you just imagine Ms. Prim and Proper here taking her wrath out on the track?"

"Definitely," Leo said.

Pride swelled in Rosie's chest. It sounded *fun*. She would need some *fun* when Leo left.

"You okay?" Leo whispered in her ear.

She nodded, even though she wasn't.

"Come help me set off firecrackers. I have those variety packs to get through."

She let Leo lead her toward the front yard, ignoring

the catcalls of her friends. They skirted the corner of Robin's house. Leo stopped as soon as they were alone and pinned her against the brick.

"Hi," he said.

"Hi."

"You look gorgeous tonight. It's turning me on."

She blushed. She'd donned a lightweight chambray dress and red lipstick. Very prim and proper, per Wren's description, but she felt pretty.

"Show me how much," she said, slipping into her disciplinarian voice. Leo's eyes went wide and his breath stuttered.

She knew he wouldn't disappoint her. He gently took her hand and placed it over the front of his jeans. His cock plumped against her palm, so she fondled him.

"Look at me," she ordered. He did. "This is mine tonight."

"Yes."

"Kiss me."

He did.

He kissed her as if the world was about to fracture around them, all eager, rushed, and desperate. She pulled back with a smile.

Leo slipped his hand into hers, and they walked to the front of the house. There was a small crowd setting off fireworks on the hot asphalt of the street.

Rosie hadn't played with fireworks in years. In fact, she couldn't remember the last time she'd held a lit punk in her hand. Maybe high school?

Leo handed her a packet of M-80s. "Blow some shit up for me, beautiful."

Rosie waited until the road had cleared before she stepped forward. She placed two fat red sticks on the ground, their green fuses touching. Then she lit them, hurrying away as soon as the fuses sparked.

She reached Leo right before the M-80s blew, and he was watching her face as the firecrackers detonated in tandem. Adrenaline flushed through her. Her heart shot to her throat. Her laughter rang out, and Leo caught her in his arms.

And that was when she remembered.

The last time she'd set off fireworks had been with him on the riverbank, a week before he'd left. Thirteen years later, he was passing her a bag of smoke bombs, and she was certain he remembered too. She didn't want this moment to end.

The night continued on. Rosie played more cornhole and spoke with Robin and Wren about roller derby. She plied Dean for stories about Leo. She observed people eating the jam she'd brought, a sense of accomplishment flowing through her. She watched William O'Dare dote on her brother. She sat with Sasha beside the pool, their feet in the water, and didn't have to talk at all.

Once the hot sun fully sunk below the horizon and the sky turned from pink to lilac to dark navy blue, everyone moved their lawn chairs into the front yard to view the partygoers' big finale. She sat on Leo's lap and pretended that life could be like this all the time.

It was everything she'd been searching for. Happiness and passion and a full heart.

Fireworks exploded over their heads, but she closed her eyes, listening to the crackle and powerful booms, feeling the reverberation of each blast in her chest.

"Rosie," Leo whispered in her ear.

"Yeah?"

"Thank you."

"For what?"

He rested his chin on her shoulder. "For giving us this time together."

Pain flared through her as bright and violent as the fireworks above their heads. They'd never said goodbye thirteen years ago. One day, he'd told her he was leaving, kissed her, and left. She'd known she would never see him again. She'd nursed her pain alone and moved on because she knew they'd done the right thing.

Now she'd received this time with him, a gift she'd never expected.

She didn't want to say goodbye.

Summer of Rosie: Take #9. Nursing a broken heart.

"Let's pretend," she said.

"Pretend what?"

"That you're not leaving tomorrow." It was such a whimsical, illogical desire. She wasn't one for whimsy as a rule, but the whole day had been colored by this fog of unreality.

His body tightened under her, but he said, "Whatever you want. Your wish. My command."

AFTER THE AMATEUR FIREWORKS SHOW, party guests started to clear out, including Rosie's siblings. Anticipation spread through her until she was practically pulsing from it. She wasn't sure how a barbecue transformed into a sex party. Would Madame Ballcrusher stand on her patio table, drop a white flag, and say, "ready, set, go"?

It still felt like a barbecue, to be honest. That was, until Rosie noticed two women kissing in the pool. One of them untied the other's bikini top. Rosie's face flamed. She glanced around. Was it rude to watch them? She'd met them earlier in the night but couldn't remember their names.

She escaped to a secluded pergola with a huge outdoor sectional inside. Leo was there talking to Dean and eating a cherry Popsicle. He smiled and tossed his hair out of his face.

She stepped to his side, and he threw an arm around her waist as he finished his snack. Rosie tried to surreptitiously take a head count of how many people were left. Eight or nine, maybe? A satisfied laugh came from the other side of the backyard.

Her head was full of hazy lust and confusion. Leo positioned her in front of him, but she was too distracted to figure out why. Then Dean nudged her chin so she was facing him.

"Do you trust me, Rosie?" Leo said in her ear.

She nodded. Dean was looking at her with hunger in his eyes.

Leo kissed the nape of her neck and trailed his lips down her spine until he reached the back of her dress. Her knees threatened to buckle. "I want to make you feel good. You want that?"

"Yes."

"I want other people to make you feel good too. Is that okay?"

She gulped. Dean was still holding her chin. She stared up at him. He was taller than her and Leo. "Just Dean?" she asked.

"Do you want it to only be me and Dean? You're in charge here."

Her pulse tripped over itself. This might be the only chance she ever got. She wasn't going to waste it. "No."

Dean grabbed her hand, pressed a kiss to her palm, and said, "I'll be right back."

Once he was gone, air left Rosie's lungs in a rush.

Leo turned her around. "You can say stop at any time."

"I know."

"I want to worship you. I want to serve you. Make you feel like nothing exists but your own pleasure."

She started to tremble. She was overwhelmed. "I don't think I can take charge," she admitted. "I don't know what I'm doing."

He sat down on the huge sofa and scooted back so she could sit between his spread legs. She leaned back against his chest.

"You don't have to do anything but close your eyes and enjoy. You can boss me around later."

So that was what she did. She closed her eyes and let him kiss her neck and trace his fingers over her skin. As Leo's palm reached her thigh, she felt someone else's presence.

"You can keep your eyes closed," Leo whispered. "It's safe." She nodded. A mouth touched her knee, and she jumped. The scratch of stubble lit up her nerve endings. A warm breeze washed over her, bringing the scent of earth and fireworks and chlorine. It was the smell of summer.

Leo tipped her head back against his shoulder and someone kissed her. Their lips were soft and smooth. Sweet in a demanding way. Rosie had to steady herself. She reached a hand out and encountered strappy leather and smooth skin, and she knew exactly who was kissing her.

Needy, greedy hands slipped inside her dress. She wasn't wearing panties, so she felt delightfully exposed. The sound of kissing and touching drifted around her. She was most aware of Leo as he wrestled his shirt off. She settled back against him. Someone slipped the strap of her dress down and licked over the peak of her shoulder. Leo groaned, and she echoed him.

It was a whirlwind of sensation. Hands on her. Then fingers inside her. Lips on her. Tongues.

She was drenched in it, in the moment. In the mouth at her breast, delicately pulling her dress and bra out of the way. In the pair of heads between her legs, touching her and kissing. In Leo, whispering in her ear, telling her she was beautiful and powerful.

She kept her eyes closed, even as she felt someone tense at her side and grunt, the slap of jerking off filling the air. She reached for them. They grasped her hand, and put it on their cock.

"Oh God," she said, the heat searing her palm.

Leo kissed her ear. "That's it, Rosie."

Leo's cock was a hard bar against her back, trapped in his jeans. She hadn't known what to expect of group sex, but this messy half-dressed pile of hedonism was far exceeding her wildest dreams.

The cock in her hand spilled over her fingers. A different mouth cleaned up the come.

She arched, a low thrum of desire spreading through her veins. Leo reached over her hip and touched her slick folds. His thumb strummed against her clit, insistent and familiar. She turned her face into his neck.

She didn't know who was touching her, or how many people, but it was his fingers that made her come. It was his arms that held her as she gasped and tipped over the edge. It was his love that had made this possible.

This moment—having so many hands and mouths on her—had been her fantasy for so long. She'd expected it to be exciting and overwhelming. She hadn't expected to feel treasured. To feel loved.

And it was all Leo.

*Leo, Leo, Leo.*

She wanted to say his name until it burned her mouth. Until it was branded inside her.

Once the pleasure arcing through her had subsided, she was almost scared to open her eyes. What if the illusion was shattered? What if this warmth in her chest, this love washing through her, disappeared now that she'd come? People moved around her. Kissing each other. Touching. She risked a glance.

She caught a flash of Dean and a woman kissing each other between her legs. Dean's hand was still gripping Rosie's thigh. Rosie found the illusion wasn't shattered at all. It was just as strong with her eyes open. The adoration and affection she felt for the people around her was overwhelming.

"You okay?" Leo asked in her ear.

"Yes."

Everyone was entwined and absorbed in each other as if they were intentionally giving Rosie a beat to catch her breath, with the exception of Leo and Robin.

Robin leaned in and very delicately kissed Rosie's mouth before pulling back, her thumb on Rosie's bottom lip.

"I'm glad you're here, friend," Robin said.

Was it that simple? Rosie hoped so.

Then Robin reached down and fisted Dean's hair. He groaned and tipped his head back. His partner grinned. The whole action and reaction couldn't have taken more than three seconds, but Rosie felt like she'd seen Robin transform into *Lady Robin* before her eyes. It was unnerving and incredibly hot.

"I want to play with you," Robin said. She winked at

the other woman. Dean nodded. "Good. Come on, then."

They both followed behind her like ducklings.

"Wow," Rosie said as they walked away. She turned in Leo's lap until she was straddling him. His chest was sweat streaked, his tattoos shining in the dim lights scattered around the patio. "That was unreal."

"You liked it?"

"I loved it." She rested her weight on him, and he grunted, a sexy, pained sound. "Oh, baby. Are you hurting?"

She tugged open his fly and plucked a condom out of her own pocket. Dresses with pockets really were the best.

With as little fanfare as possible, she sheathed him and sat on his cock. Her dress spread out around them, obscuring them. If it weren't for Leo's reaction, probably no one would have known they were fucking.

Her pussy was still throbbing from her orgasm, and it felt so good to have him hard and rough inside her. She moved slowly, grinding. Other people were watching them, but she didn't want to look away from Leo's face. His pleasure seemed excruciating.

He buried his face in her sweaty neck. The world melted away as Leo fell to pieces in her arms.

"Can I?" he begged. "Please, Rosie, can I?"

"Yes." She kissed his temple, his ear, the curve of his neck. "Yes."

"Oh fuck."

His cock pulsed as he came inside her, and she felt

triumphant. She'd stripped this wonderful man down to sensation. He'd given her gratification and love, and she'd returned it. This was so much better than she'd anticipated. It was more than she'd expected when they'd agreed to that silly sex list. It felt inevitable and incredible and *honest*. Like they'd become their truest selves in each other's arms.

## Chapter Thirteen

The stars winked through the slats of the pergola, and Leo wanted to drown in them. His body was tired and sated.

Rosie gave him a kiss, swung herself off his lap, and informed him that she needed to pee and find her antibiotics because "she refused to get a UTI after the best night of sex ever."

Leo laughed and went to clean himself up. A lot of the remaining partygoers had paired off, so Robin's house was mostly quiet. He found his way to his favorite part of Robin's backyard. It was this huge U-shaped cushioned bench overlooking the bluff and surrounded by plush green grass. There were small solar lamps planted around the base of the bench and strings of lights in the trees nearby. He couldn't see the river. The gulf below was pure darkness. It felt beautiful and dangerous. The bluff's edge gave him that itchy feeling, the one that pushed him to jump in his truck and race toward the next exciting thing. He had wondered if his newly unearthed feelings for Rosie would stem that flood. They hadn't, but the impulse was different now. He felt the desire to fly, to search out the next muse, to run, but he wanted a tether. A home base. A connection and a soft place to land. He wanted a partner to go on adventures with, a partner to call at the end of the day. He wanted Rosie. She was the piece of his heart that he would always return to.

She found him a few minutes later. She was barefoot, and her hair glowed golden in the moonlight.

"How you doing, sweetness?" he asked her, pitching his voice deep and silly.

She laughed, that laugh he loved, the one that was so rare. "Oh, I'm fabulous."

She curled up on his lap, and he pressed his face into her hair. She smelled like honey and sex. It was intoxicating.

"Want to talk about it?"

"About what?" she asked.

"The fact that you just had sex with five people."

"Was that how many there were?"

He chuckled. She seemed so unbothered by it, which was good. He didn't want her to regret it.

"It was amazing. I ..." She shook her head. "Having you there made it extraordinary. It was special."

"It was. You are."

She sighed, a deep contented thing that settled his fears. She might want this to be only a summer fling, but he was willing to let those concerns drift away on the wind.

A whisper of footsteps sounded behind them. Leo could tell it was Dean. He recognized the gait, and he couldn't imagine anyone else seeking him out. Dean usually sought him out.

Dean smiled at Leo gently, but there was a tinge of sadness there. He was shirtless and had claw marks on his chest.

"Hi, you two," Dean said. Rosie's head snapped up. She evidently hadn't realized they'd attracted a visitor.

"Hello." Rosie sat up straight. Dean seemed a little wary, like he wasn't sure if he was welcome. Rosie reached a hand out to him and he took it, relief stark on his face.

He plopped down next to Leo, sprawling his long legs out, and the three of them rested in silence. On the horizon, dozens of amateur fireworks shows played out. Some farther away than others, nothing more than distant sprays of light.

After a few minutes, Rosie glanced at Dean, and Leo followed her gaze. Dean's eyes were closed, like he was asleep.

She started to whisper in Leo's ear, telling him all the things she still wanted to try. All the ways he turned her on. He shifted, need rushing through him at her words, at her fantasies. When she asked Leo if he was on board, he nodded.

"Dean?" she murmered.

"Hmm?"

"You're a very handsome man," she said.

Dean grinned and opened his eyes. "You want to ask me something, Rosie?"

She smiled back. It was sharp. "I want Leo to ask you something."

Rather than *asking* outright, Leo leaned in and kissed Dean on the mouth. Dean cupped his cheek. There was a lot of familiarity between them, but this, with Rosie there, would be new.

"Will you fuck me?" Leo said against Dean's lips.

Dean pulled back. "For Rosie? You gonna watch us?" he asked her.

"If you'll let me."

In response, Dean stood and shucked off his shorts. Rosie handed him lube and a condom from her magical dress pockets.

Leo's head spun. Rosie slipped off his lap and pushed him up and out of his seat. Dean stripped Leo of his clothes.

In no time, he was on his knees in the grass, facing Rosie from about six feet away with Dean directly behind him. Dean opened him up quickly with his fingers. They'd done this dance before.

"Oh God," he moaned as Dean brushed against his prostate. He almost slammed his eyes shut, but he didn't because Rosie was watching him, and he wanted to watch her right back.

Her breath was rising and falling rapidly, her breasts straining the bodice of her dress. He knew she wasn't wearing panties, and the moment she shifted her legs restlessly, he felt it in his whole body.

Finally, Dean placed his cock at Leo's entrance. Leo cried out as Dean thrust inside. That insistent press burned him up. Dean held him with an arm over his torso and one at his hip, keeping him exposed for Rosie.

He loved to be fucked, no doubt about it, but this time was different. His entire body felt taken over.

Dean grunted and bit into the side of Leo's neck, and that lick of pain sent pulses of pleasure to his balls. He ached everywhere. He stared up into Rosie's eyes and reached for his cock.

"Nope," she said softly, popping the *P*.

"Oh fuck," he gasped.

Dean chuckled darkly behind him.

Rosie crossed her legs sedately, and Leo about died. This was too hot. She looked like a principal waiting to chastise him.

Dean's prick was a rod inside him, caressing his prostate with every move. Dean knew what he liked and was using that to his advantage. Leo trembled and clutched at the arm around his chest.

"Don't close your eyes, baby," Rosie whispered.

"Rosie," he said, his voice a broken plea. "I need, I need …"

Rosie trailed her fingers over her leg. "You need to kneel there and take it, Leo."

Dean snuck his hand from Leo's hip and fondled his balls. Leo's head hitched back as if he'd been punched.

"Rosie." He couldn't seem to stop saying her name.

"Last a bit longer and I'll reward you," she whispered.

"With what?" he managed to choke out.

"You'll see."

Dean fisted a hand over Leo's crown, and Leo had to bite the inside of his cheek to keep his orgasm at bay. His pre-come made Dean's hand smooth and slick.

"That's it, Leo," Rosie said, after what felt like an hour of perfect torture, but was probably only a minute. "Good boy."

His body started to seize at those words, but Dean gripped the base of his cock hard to stop the onslaught.

There was an extended beat of silence where no one moved. Rosie obviously knew he'd almost come, and that the only thing that had stopped it was Dean.

She smiled. "Close enough. You want to see my tits or my cunt?"

"Oh my fucking God," Leo groaned.

Dean licked his ear and whispered, "You need to marry her. She's an angel."

Laughter threatened to bubble up from inside him, but he was too turned on to make a sound other than to growl, "Cunt."

"Great choice," Rosie said. She lifted her dress up and over her head. She was wearing a ruby red bra and her skin was silvery in the darkness. She spread her legs, and she was wet and glistening.

She touched herself and hummed. "Are you ready to come?"

Leo nodded, but he couldn't form words. He couldn't take his eyes off her as she played her fingers over her clit. She was smiling. He loved her. He loved her so much. His heart was a bottle rocket, pointed right at her.

"Go ahead."

Leo cried out and shot, thick and hot, all over himself and Dean's palm.

Dean's hands grasped at Leo's body desperately as he followed him over.

Rosie stopped touching herself. She gripped the edge of the bench, her knuckles white and legs splayed. Leo tumbled forward, out of Dean's arms and crawled toward her. He pressed his face against her thigh and breathed.

She brushed her fingers through his hair. He wanted to tell her that he loved her. Instead, he wrenched her legs apart and worshiped her.

She twisted against his lips and shattered almost immediately. The fact that watching him get fucked by someone else had turned her on was a revelation. He climbed into her lap and fell headlong into her embrace. Dean dropped kisses on both their cheeks, whispering something in Rosie's ear, then left.

Leo kept kissing her until no fireworks lit the sky and most of the world had gone to sleep. He kissed her like he was running out of time, because he was.

## Chapter Fourteen

Rosie woke up alone in Leo's bed—a bed that smelled like lemons and the smoke from last night's fireworks. It wasn't unusual for her to awaken without someone by her side. At least, she tried to tell herself that. She'd been sleeping alone for over a year, and the other day, she'd roused to find Leo on the phone outside rather than in bed. He was an early riser, and in the summer, she was *not*.

She didn't know why his absence hurt this morning.

When she walked out of his bedroom, she found him preparing his Airstream for travel, and all the pain she'd been holding at bay hit her in one fell swoop.

Leo glanced up, regret in his eyes.

"What time do you need to leave?" she asked him, trying to whittle this interaction down to logistics. She was good at logistics.

"In about an hour to make it before dark. I promised

my parents I'd stop by their house on my way out as well."

Something must have passed over her face, something she was trying to hide, because he stepped toward her.

"I can stay. Not for a lot longer, but I can stay. We could have lunch. I could—"

"No, it's fine. I don't want you to be driving too late."

Leo's eyes tracked over her, and she shuttered her emotions. He hauled her into his lounge area and sat with her on the same seat where they'd first reconnected. The place where he'd drawn her.

"I don't want this to end," he said.

"I already told you, it doesn't have to. We can fuck when you come to town."

He traced his fingers up her thigh. This felt like a breakup.

Why did this feel like a breakup? She was pretty sure he was about to tell her the opposite. Dean's words from the night before prickled the back of her mind. She pushed them away.

"This is hard for me," he said. She nodded, too choked by panic to respond. "I'm going to tell you exactly what I want. You don't need to respond. Hell, you can just take it in, and we can discuss it over the phone tomorrow. Or in a few weeks. I'll wait for you to decide. I'd wait a really long time for you."

"Best get it out, then." Her voice sounded cold. She hated that her voice sounded cold.

He smiled as if he saw straight through her façade. "I

want to be together. I want us to be in a relationship. Permanent. A pair. I want to be your person."

Her heart was pounding. "How would that work?"

He slipped her hands between his. She clutched at his fingers.

"We do a mix of long distance and in person. I would still travel, because it's part of who I am and my job requires it, to a degree. Maybe sometimes you come with me, especially in the summer. But then, during the school year, I come home as much as possible. I've been searching for a home for a long time. I think I was trying to find my way back here. To you."

This was a lot. Her Summer of Rosie had gone off the rails, what with the orgies, the jam, the pegging, and this barrage of *feelings*.

"That's ... unexpected. What would a long-distance relationship look like with you?" Her mind latched onto the mechanics rather than the heart of what he was telling her. He wanted to *be with her*. "Would we keep in touch? Would you sleep with other people?"

"We'd keep in touch. We'd talk every day. We'd come up with a routine that works for us. Our own routine. Calls in the morning and video chats at night. Lots of phone sex. We could be connected even if we aren't physically together. And as for sex with other people, we make our own rules. I don't have any desire to have sex that doesn't involve you, but I'm open to whatever you want."

He kissed her palm, and tears threatened to spring to her eyes.

Stupid tears.

Stupid feelings.

"I don't intend to take your independence from you," Leo continued. "I don't want to change you or upset the security you've worked so hard for. I want to be a source of security *for* you. We could be *secure* in our relationship, even when we're not in the same place. You could be *secure* in the knowledge that I will forever be on my way back to you."

The type of security that Leo spoke of—it wasn't at all how Rosie had expected her life to be thirteen years ago. She'd wanted the nest. The home. The steady job and steady husband. She'd needed to be close to her siblings. That was how she'd viewed security.

Now she wasn't so sure. It was appealing, this proposition of Leo's, but was it realistic? She was too much of a pragmatist to trust it.

"I didn't anticipate this," she said. Her voice was stilted. She grimaced. "I don't know, Leo."

"You can think about it." He held her face in his hands. He was shaking.

She loved him. That wasn't the problem.

The problem was that she'd never imagined that this type of relationship—something a bit unconventional, a bit strange—would work for her. She had always been steady, boring Rosie. It was hard to move on from that self-perception, though moving on had been the whole point of taking this summer for herself.

"I don't want to leave my job," she said. "And I like my condo."

"I'm not asking you to leave either, Rosie. I love your

condo. I want to help you make the backyard your own oasis. Maybe one day it could be a place that feels like home to me too ... if you wanted."

"This is a lot." She felt overwhelmed. "There's not enough room to make jam in your Airstream."

As soon as she said that, she flushed. She wasn't married to jam making, for heaven's sake, but it was easier to address the silly stuff than the big stuff.

"If that's your only issue with my proposition, then we're doing pretty good."

"I need to think." She gently nudged Leo out of her space and stood. She turned back toward him, a zip of anger rushing through her. "You were supposed to help me work through a sex checklist, not upend my life, Leo."

He held up his hands. "I know. Rosie, I know, but I ... I don't want to lose you, and it was never just sex to me. I lo—"

"Oh my God. Don't say that right now. Wait until I'm not freaking out."

A slow, devastating smile stretched across his face. His stubble sparkled in the morning sun slipping through the window, tinges of red mixing with the dark brown. He was so handsome. No man should be allowed to be that handsome.

"But I can say it when you're not freaking out?"

"Maybe. I need to go." She had champagne poppers exploding in her chest. She had to get out of there. She needed time to calm down and examine what was best for her without the distraction of flight or fight.

"Take as long as you need. I'm not in a hurry, Rosie Posey."

"Don't call me that."

He ignored her huffiness. "I'll be in Memphis for a week, and then I'll be wherever you want me to be."

"Fine. Okay."

He stood and wrapped her in his arms. She wanted to cry.

"This isn't the end unless you want it to be the end," he said.

She pressed her forehead into his throat and didn't respond. As much as she had hoped that the Summer of Rosie would make her more spontaneous and open to change, she was still the reserved woman who needed time to study and consider and weigh her options.

And yet, Leo wanted her.

"I'm not going to say goodbye," she whispered against his skin.

"Good." His voice was fierce. "Can I have a kiss before I leave?"

She threaded her fingers into his hair. She could tell he expected her to overwhelm him with a kiss, to drown him with it. Instead, she kissed him lightly. Gently.

Lovingly.

Fuck.

He said her name against her lips, like an impulse or a primordial instinct. She touched his face—skimmed her fingertips over his eyebrows, along his stubbled jaw, around his lip piercing—trying to memorize it.

"I have something for you," he said. He handed her a

big bundle wrapped in crisp brown craft paper. "Be gentle with it."

She nodded, kissed him one last time, and left.

———————

ROSIE DIDN'T MAKE it two blocks before she called Sasha.

"Leo's leaving for Memphis today," Rosie said conversationally as if it wasn't a huge damn deal.

"Do you wanna fuck some shit up? Or do you want emergency brunch?"

"How in the world would we fuck shit up?" Rosie asked.

"I could find a bunch of breakable stuff, and you could go to town on it with a bat. I've seen that on TV," Sasha said.

"Oh my. I'd need protective equipment. Safety glasses and gloves."

Sasha laughed. "I love you, Rosie. I'll see you at brunch." She hung up.

Rosie sighed. She hadn't wanted this to devolve into their normal sibling séance. She'd wanted to vent a little in the privacy of her own vehicle. She was used to helping Sasha and Benji figure their issues out. It was part of her oldest-sister role. The reverse made her uncomfortable.

Still, she made the fifteen-minute drive to Jolly's Café and parked in the almost empty parking lot. She was pretty sure the Holiday family was the only thing keeping this place in business.

Before going inside, she decided to open the present Leo had given her.

She regretted it instantly.

On top was the sketch he'd done of her that first day. He'd added to it. There were small flushes of color on her cheeks, bra, and shorts. Then there was his book, *Lovers*.

She opened it to the title page to find a huge paragraph of his messy script. Her heart started hammering in her throat. Maybe she should wait to read it until after emergency brunch. She had a feeling it was going to rip her to pieces.

She didn't have that much self-control, though. Her eyes sped over the paragraph, skimming it once before slowing down and taking it in.

He had written, "I believe that art is a life raft. It connects us and keeps us afloat. It saves our lives. It saved mine. A year ago, I had a memory of you dancing through a cloud of smoke bombs. You were eighteen, and I didn't want to say goodbye. I couldn't shake that memory. I started dreaming in pastel colors. In pale pinks and powdery blues and soft yellows. It was all I thought about. Those colors surrounding someone I loved. This book bloomed from that memory. You're my life raft. You always have been. And I'll always love you. —Leo"

"Oh my God."

She was crying, which pissed her off to no end, but she couldn't seem to stop. She unwrapped the last parcel.

It was a watercolor painting of that moment by the

river thirteen years ago. The one she'd remembered last night when she'd been setting off fireworks. She'd lined up a bag of smoke bombs, lit them all at once, and skipped through the smoke to land in Leo's lap. She had drunk from his sour-cherry snow cone and kissed him like he wasn't about to break her heart.

It was there, on the canvas in her hands. Billows of colorful smoke and her shadow peeking through it, vague and nebulous and haunting. Most people wouldn't look at this painting and see her, but she recognized herself in the angle of her shoulders and the way her feet were planted in the sand.

There was a lot of love in this painting.

Leo loved her, and she'd let him drive away.

A loud banging on her car window made her jump and almost drop her precious present. She glanced over to see Benji blinking at her through the glass, his eyes shocked. He tried to open her door, but it was locked. He knocked again.

Rosie pushed open the door, and Benji pulled her out of the car. He checked her over as if he expected to see a physical sign of why she was crying.

"What did he do?" Benji demanded. She laughed.

Sasha parked her completely ridiculous VW Bug next to them and vaulted out of the front seat. She rushed over.

"What did he do?" she asked.

"Oh my God," Rosie said. She was laughing and kind of crying and she loved her siblings so much. "Let's go inside."

Benji and Sasha were handling her like fine china. She sat down next to Sasha in their normal booth. They ordered for her and pushed a mimosa into her hand.

The waitress did not seem surprised to see one of the Holiday siblings having a breakdown. Old hat, this. It made Rosie laugh harder.

"What's happening?" Benji whispered to Sasha. Sasha shook her head.

"He loves me," Rosie blurted out.

Silence followed that statement. She noticed Benji and Sasha sharing very concerned looks. Rosie threw back her mimosa and poured herself another one.

"That sounds horrible," Benji said, obviously unsure how to handle this. "Fuck that guy?" Rosie felt Sasha kick Benji under the table. He held up his hands. "What? She's acting weird."

"Do you think my emotions are all over the place because of the orgy?" Rosie asked.

More silence.

"I shouldn't have asked that," she said into the awkwardness.

Benji—the *lingerie influencer*—was holding his hand over his mouth, and Sasha—the *sex-toy saleswoman*—was blushing. Rosie didn't know why they were acting prudish now.

"Okay, let's start at the beginning," Sasha said. "Tell us what happened."

Rosie took another gulp of mimosa and did. She told them about the nude modeling and the sex checklist and the art and the jam making and his mother and the pesky way her heart hurt and a PG-13 executive summary of the orgy and, lastly, the proposition he'd made that morning and the absolutely heart-wrenching gifts he'd given her.

"Oh, so he's Prince Charming. I see," Benji said once Rosie was done. "What's the issue?"

"What's the issue?" Rosie said. Or maybe she screeched it.

Both her siblings stared.

"I can't …" What? She couldn't what? Figure out how to live a perfectly happy life with a wonderful man who, oh yeah, she was madly in love with? "I can't live in a trailer half the year."

Benji rolled his spoiled little eyes.

"Watch it, bub," Rosie spat. "I will tell William that you slept with a baby blankie until you were eighteen."

Sasha took Rosie's hands in her own and pulled her focus from their younger brother. "Okay, most important question: Do you love him?"

"Yes, but—"

"No buts, Rosie. You love him."

"Love isn't everything. My divorce is proof of that."

Benji raised his hand as if he were a kindergartener asking for permission to speak.

"What?" she growled.

He bit his lip, uncertainty flashing in his eyes. "You once told me that the right love makes you the best version of yourself. For you, that meant it would be full of wonder, affection, and discovery. Do you remember that?"

Of course she remembered that. It had only been five months ago when he'd been having his own love crisis with William.

"Yes," she said reluctantly.

"Does this love feel like that?"

She finished her mimosa. Rather than answering him, she said, "All I've ever wanted is to be settled. I'm worried this will upset that."

"I don't think it will," Sasha jumped in. "He's just asking for a new normal. For both of you."

"What if you guys need me? If I'm spending my summers traipsing all over the country with Leo, I won't be able to be there for you, and I—"

"Whoa there, Ms. Thing. We're not your children or your students," Sasha said. "We're your adult siblings. I know you've got the responsibility bug, but that's not a good reason to stop living your life. That's what this whole Summer of Rosie experiment was about. Living. Your. Life. You need to turn that shit off."

Tears pooled in Rosie's eyes again. She tried to brush them away, but not before she saw alarm on Sasha and Benji's faces.

"It's not that easy."

Benji reached across the table for her hand. She gave it to him. "I'll always need my older sisters. I'll always need you. Nothing will change that, but you can't let your hot erotic artist go because you like cleaning up my messes."

Rosie poured herself more mimosa.

"Okay, I think you need to eat your pancakes first,"

Sasha said, plucking the plastic champagne flute from her hand.

"So, again," Benji said. "Does this love with Leo tear you up inside? Does it hurt you? Or does it make you your best self?"

Rosie's heart was going wild in her chest. She thought back to William telling her that she was made of sturdier stuff and Dean whispering in her ear that he'd never seen a better match than her and Leo. She thought about the way these six days with Leo had made her happier than she had ever been. She had been able to discover things about herself that she'd never thought possible. Like how much she enjoyed pegging.

"Yes," she said finally. She loved him, and it didn't hurt. Not anymore.

Benji clapped his hands. "Great. Now, you need to grand gesture him. It's the only way."

Rosie shot out of her seat. She wobbled. "Grand gestures are not my style."

"But that's the best part of making up," Benji whined.

She waved him off and turned to her sister. "Can you drive me? I think I'm drunk."

Sasha smiled. "Where?"

"Somewhere between here and Memphis."

## Chapter Fifteen

L uckily, Leo had not made it to Memphis. In fact, as Rosie discovered, he'd only made it a hundred miles by the time she called him and ordered him to stay put. He obliged by waiting for her at a rest stop on the interstate.

By the time Sasha pulled into the rest-stop parking lot, Rosie had sobered up and was about to come out of her skin.

She didn't wait for Sasha to say anything but jumped out of the car and wrestled her two suitcases from Sasha's ridiculously small backseat. Rosie watched from the corner of her eye as Leo stepped out of his Airstream.

Sasha rolled down her window and handed over the big jar of sun pickles that Rosie had left on the car's floor. "Want me to wait?"

"No."

"What if this doesn't go the way you want it to?"

Rosie glanced at Leo. He was leaning back against

that silver bullet of a trailer looking for all the world like a model for bad-boy jeans. Damn, she loved him.

"It will." Rosie leaned in and kissed her sister's cheek. "Love you. Don't forget to water my succulents." She patted the top of Sasha's Bug and carried her suitcases toward her future.

"Fancy meeting you here," Leo said. His eyes followed Sasha's car as it zoomed off.

"You got room for one more in there?" she asked. "I packed light. This is mostly jam-making supplies and sex toys."

He took a tentative step toward her, then a faster one. She dropped her suitcases and gingerly placed the pickles on the cement. He swept her into his arms.

There was a field of golden wheat to their right and a highway full of fast cars to their left. The summer sun was lemon bright, and Leo's hands were strong. It felt very cinematic.

He picked her up and swung her around, his happiness this visceral, palpable thing. She wrapped her legs around his waist and kissed him.

"I brought you pickles," she said.

He didn't put her down. He hugged her harder.

"Leo, say something."

"Can't. Think I'm gonna cry."

She kissed his ear. "Because of the pickles?"

He put her down and caught her face between his palms. He opened his mouth to speak, but she stopped him.

"Hold on. Me first." She gripped his wrists. "I love you. Okay, your turn."

Leo's forehead started to crumple, and he shook his head. "I thought you might decide that you didn't …"

"Didn't what?"

"Want me." He shrugged. "I've been crying and listening to my Lilith Fair playlist for two hours, trying to wash my emotions away. Didn't work. I was so scared I'd lost you. I was sure I was making a mistake by leaving."

She grabbed his hand and turned it over so she could see his tattoo, the one that said *Life Raft*. "We've both been adrift for a while now. I want to be your life raft. I want you to be mine. I want everything you said. The split time. The summer trips in your Airstream. The school year at my condo. I want to make jam with you, and go to leather conventions with you, and have way too much phone sex with you. I will never try to change you or hold you back. I want you to know that even when we're apart, I still love you, I understand you, and I'll be waiting for you at the end of the road."

"I don't want this relationship to hurt you. Ever. I've hurt people in the past. My schedule and the traveling. It's not easy on people, and I—"

She put her hand over his mouth. "Don't make me get bossy. I'm not your past. You're not mine. We're not the same people we were at eighteen, thank God. Most importantly, I don't want to change you. Will it be hard? Of course. Does that mean it's not worth the fight? No. It is worth it. You're worth it, Leo."

Tears starred his eyelashes, and she couldn't hold in her grin. He tried to blink them away. It didn't work.

"I love you," she said again. She moved her hand off his lips.

He laughed. "Shit."

"You can say it back now."

"You'll allow it, huh?"

"Yes." She smiled and stepped back, primly brushing her hands over her dress.

He pointed at her. "Rosie Posey, I love the fuck out of you."

She frowned. "Don't call me that."

"You like it."

"I do." She rolled her eyes.

He reeled her back in. "What now?"

"Memphis. I've made a whole list of things to do while we're there. Summer of Rosie: Part Deux."

He kissed along her throat. "That doesn't surprise me. Your lists are the best. They sometimes lead to orgies."

"Well, this one leads to Graceland."

"I'll take it."

Leo loaded Rosie's bags into the Airstream, put the jar of pickles in the backseat of his truck, and helped her into the passenger's seat.

"You don't mind being the passive passenger today?" he asked her. She laughed, remembering that she'd told him she wasn't into that on the first day they'd reconnected.

She pulled out her phone. "No. I'll direct you." She grinned. "I know you like that."

"Good God, Rosie." He pressed his face against her sternum and she brushed her fingers through his hair. "I don't think I've ever been this happy."

She put her lips to his temple. "Just you wait."

They hit the road and followed the summer sun.

## Epilogue

---

TWO YEARS LATER

The sun glimmered on the edges of the horizon. An impatient party a mile away shot off their nighttime fireworks even though it wasn't yet dark. The sound reached Leo, a distant crackle on the breeze.

"It's hot today," Rosie said. She had her hair in two stubby braids to keep it off her face. It made her look innocent.

She was not.

"You can skinny dip in the river to cool off. I'll keep watch," Leo said with a bit of a leer.

They had a whole picnic spread out on the bank of the river. They'd had the option to spend the Fourth of July at Robin's annual barbecue but had opted for their own celebration. It had been three weeks since they'd seen each other, and Leo was greedy for Rosie's time.

"What would you do if I took you up on that dare? You'd be shocked," she said starchily.

"I would be. Blow something up for me. It turns me on."

She grinned and picked up a bottle rocket and a plastic Coca-Cola bottle. It took her a few minutes to arrange the bottle and rocket safely.

He was a lucky son of a bitch. He had the love of his life within arm's reach, and that was a blessing.

Fifteen years ago, they'd played with smoke bombs on this same stretch of sand. He'd been so scared to say goodbye.

He still didn't like to say goodbye. They focused on their hellos instead.

Rosie used a punk to light the bottle rocket. She rushed away from the sparking fuse. The rocket zipped into the air, whistling loudly. Rosie sucked in a noisy breath. There was excitement and delight in her eyes.

"Come here, love," he said.

She crashed into his arms. "I'm so happy you're here."

"Me too."

She always said that when they were together. It was hard sometimes, just like they knew it would be, but they spent more time with each other than apart, and the separation made every reunion sweeter.

Nighttime fell around them as they snacked on cherry jam and homemade bread. Crickets and toads sang on the shoreline and lightning bugs blinked around them. The sky twinkled with stars.

Leo was content. He was exactly where he was meant to be. Nothing clawing at his chest, pulling him in a different direction. His only impulse was to move toward the next adventure with this woman by his side.

She held his hand and waited out his silence. He loved her so much the emotion felt too big for his body.

With the darkness came more fireworks until the sky was blazing with rockets, showers of dazzling lights, and blooming colors. There were multiple shows going on around them, close but not too close.

He kissed Rosie lightly on the lips, then tumbled her onto her back on their picnic blanket. She was wearing jean shorts, so he wrestled those off her. She didn't put up a fight.

As he slipped her panties into his pocket, he noticed a large mark on her hip.

"What's this from, Prim Reaper?" he asked, using her roller derby name.

"It's a fishnet burn."

He kissed it. She was proud of her bumps and bruises, so he worshiped them.

After a few seconds, she'd obviously gotten impatient, because she said, "*Leo*," in the bossy teacher voice he loved.

"Yes, ma'am?"

She grabbed him by his hair and shoved his face toward her pussy. "Hurry up."

He laughed and nuzzled against her. This was a risk, though no one had ever disturbed them at this spot. Still, she wouldn't want to be exposed for too long.

He inhaled her scent and kissed her thigh. "Watch the fireworks, Rosie. I'm here to serve."

She let out a shaky breath and relaxed.

He licked her, dragging his tongue through her folds and up to her clit. He felt the pleasure spread through her body with every twitch and twist, every gasp. He let his fingers play, dipping into her cunt.

"Fill me up," she rasped out, her voice a whisper.

He did. He followed her orders because nothing in the world made him happier.

Her eyes flashed in the darkness, the reflection of fireworks burning in them. He watched that fireworks show through her eyes. Every burst, every bloom. The wonder and the whip of adrenaline. She detonated on his lips and hands, his own finale.

"Fuck, you're incredible at that," she gasped at last.

"Thanks. You taste good."

"Dirty boy. Take your pants off. Get on your back."

He grinned and followed orders. "Your wish. My command." Before his head hit the blanket, Rosie was on him, and he was in her, and he felt like a lit fuse.

"Your turn. Watch the fireworks," Rosie said sweetly. He knew not to trust that sugary voice. There was nothing sweet about what she was about to do. He loved it that way.

"I don't need to." He caught Rosie's hands and threaded their fingers together. "Would rather watch you."

## Author's Note

I wrote the majority of this book in February and March 2020, while the world was being turned upside down. As I dealt with the isolation, fear, anxiety, and grief so many of us experienced, a friend sent me a video of a woman singing in rural Ireland. That singer's name is Cathie Ryan. In this particular video, she talks about music being a life raft that reaches through time and space to connect us in difficult times.

That sentiment pulled me through all my personal obstacles during those months. Music is a life raft. Art is a life raft. Fiction is a life raft. And I believe love is a life raft that can reach through space, time, screens, and physical distance to connect us. I couldn't have finished this book without Cathie Ryan, or without my friend Ashley, who sent me that video to lift my spirits when I needed it most.

## Excerpt from STOCKING STUFFERS (So Over the Holidays #1)

Did you miss the first book in the So Over the Holiday series? Read on for Chapter 1 of *Stocking Stuffers*!

Sasha lifted the toy from her huge red bag with a flourish, and the jingle bells on her reindeer antlers tinkled merrily.

"This little darling, the Love Bite, is my favorite of the bunch." She displayed the toy in her hands like a model on *The Price is Right*. She'd found, after years of peddling her wares to anyone and everyone who would listen, that drama sells. Especially at Christmas. "The handle is ergonomic, and it's sturdy. Frankly, there is nothing I hate more than a flimsy sex toy."

The Staunchly Raunchy Book Club members tittered, and Sasha grinned. "Y'all know what I mean. I can tell."

Gently teasing the clients was one of Sasha's customer

service tricks. She was adept at figuring out which Lady Robin's Intimate Implements partygoers were gregarious and bantering with them. But today, Sasha's heart wasn't exactly full of holiday cheer *or* consumerism. She felt like the fake elf at the party, and she'd never been a very good faker.

"The Love Bite uses suction technology, and I swear to the Ghost of Good Orgasms Past, it's the closest to real oral I've ever found in a sex toy. You just place the head over your clit and it creates a suck-and-release sensation," she said matter-of-factly.

Sasha normally loved filling in at a Lady Robin's sales party when one of the regular reps called in sick. She loved chatting with the clients, and she definitely loved the commission money.

But she *hated* Christmas, so this party sucked.

Sasha passed the Love Bite to Valerie, the party's hostess and a beautiful femme lesbian, who tested the suction on her thumb.

"Oh, very nice," Valerie said. "I might give up the girlfriend search for this baby." She waved the Love Bite at her friends. "This is my new girlfriend now!"

Sasha couldn't hold in her professional pride. "Plus, it's waterproof."

Sasha's friend, Robin, had started Lady Robin's Intimate Implements, a boutique sex toy and lingerie company, as a pop-up shop seven years ago. Sasha had been the whole of the marketing department for the first three years before their company had exploded into a multi-city operation. They supplemented their online and local vendor sales with bridal showers and birthday parties attended by their salaried marketing reps. This was the first book club they'd been commissioned for, as far as Sasha knew. Their company had made Robin, and Sasha by extension, stockings full of cash.

A blast of wind hit the Winterberry Inn, causing the old house to creak and rattle. Sasha whipped around to see out the big bay window. It was dark out there, and she desperately hoped the expected snow and ice held off until she was home. Her darling baby—a restored 1984 VW Bug—was a disaster on icy roads.

Valerie, who owned the Winterberry Inn and was definitely the evil mastermind of the Staunchly Raunchy Book Club, called a pause on the proceedings to get everyone mulled wine and spiked eggnog. Sasha took the brief reprieve to glance around the luxurious hearth room. The inn was a cozy bed and breakfast with seemingly endless rooms and Christmas charm in every nook and cranny.

The hearth room spilled over with Christmas bobbles, garland, boxwood wreaths, and lights. A huge spruce tree, decked out in glittery gold, was activating Sasha's allergies.

Christmas made her itch, even when it was beautiful.

Maybe especially when it was beautiful.

Once the book club members were back in their circle of seats, Sasha pulled a paddle out of her bag and pasted on a fake smile.

"We don't have a huge variety of impact-play instruments, like crops or whips, but if you're in the market for that, I can give you suggestions for other vendors. We only have one paddle, but it's exceptional, if I do say so myself." She brandished the wooden paddle Robin had created for the holidays. It had a word etched into the wide, flat end. "You can personalize the word, so it could be your name or your partner's name. Other common words are *BABY* or *SLUT*. This is our Christmas edition, you know, if Santa gets you going."

The group laughed as she handed off the paddle adorned with the word *HO!* The book club members had been discussing a BDSM romance novel when she'd arrived, and the group erupted in chatter as they deliberated over whether the characters in the book would have enjoyed such play.

Sounded like they definitely would have been down.

Sasha listened to them with half an ear as she removed the last items from her bag. For a perverse second, she wished her roller bag was velvet, like Santa's, rather than boring nylon. Velvet would match the red dress she'd donned in the hopes of appearing to be a bundle of cheer.

False cheer, but whatever.

Once the room quieted down, Sasha displayed her final toys.

"Last but not least, next month we're debuting a new line called Prick Me, for the person or persons in your life with dicks and prostates, but we have a bit of stock available for purchase today. Call it a sexy sneak peek."

She waved one of the toys—a holly-green cylinder with an opening on one end. "Here is our Fancy Fleshstroker, which comes in twelve diverse skin tones and several fun colors. These have a soft, silky interior and are super easy to clean. We're also debuting two vibrating prostate massagers of differing shapes, named, quite simply, the P-Spot Pulse and Pulse 2."

She held them up and demonstrated how to turn them both on.

A quiet, earnest-looking white woman named Louise laughed. "This might sound stupid, but can you explain how those work?"

Sasha smiled, a real one this time, and put her proverbial sex-educator cap on. "So the prostate is a gland in front of the rectum in people born with penises and prostates. It has tons of pleasure sensors, so it can feel good when it's stimulated. A lot of people with prostates enjoy having theirs touched, and that isn't specific to certain sexualities. Prostate play can result in some pretty spectacular orgasms. With consent, of course, all you have to do is lube this baby up and insert it into—"

A big *thump* resounded almost directly behind her, and she dropped the toys onto the hardwood floor. Somehow, the vibrator on the Pulse 2 was activated on impact, so it buzzed and danced all over the place.

As she scrambled down to grab the toy, trying not to flash everyone since her holiday dress was *short*, Valerie shouted, "Perry! What are you doing here?"

Sasha got the toy turned off before twisting around. There was a man standing in the entryway of the room, a gym bag—evidently full of bricks considering the noise it had made when hitting the ground—by his feet.

*Hot damn.*

He was the type of man who could make her Christmas knickers twist. Tall, lean, pale, with dark curly hair and a beard. Plus, he was staring at her like she was a piece of rum cake.

She wanted to be his rum cake.

*Double damn.*

He ran a hand roughly through his hair. "I drove in a day early to beat the winter storm, which didn't work. It's already icy out there. I didn't expect to walk in on my favorite book club getting a sex-toy demo." He didn't take his eyes off Sasha.

Chuckles filled the room, and Sasha slowly stood up. No one seemed particularly perturbed about being interrupted by this man. Instead, the room was alight with excitement at his arrival. She smoothed her red velvet dress down with one hand while clutching the sex toys in the other. Her stupid antlers jingled.

Valerie waved an arm dismissively. "Well, you showed up a day early, so ..."

"So?" He was still staring at Sasha, his gaze tracking over her face.

"So maybe it's your own fault if your delicate constitution can't handle talk of prostate massagers," Sasha said with an extra dose of sass.

A grin slowly spread across his face, and dear God, he was hotter than she'd realized.

"Fair assessment. I'm sorry, we've never met. I'm Perry Winters." He finally drew his attention away from her and checked out the members of the Staunchly

Raunchy Book Club. "I think I know all the other Raunchies here, but not you."

Raunchies? Was that what they called themselves? Because that was adorable.

He stuck his hand out, and Sasha stumbled on her way over to shake it. His hand was sturdy and huge. Occasionally, Sasha loved the feel of soft, delicate hands, but Perry was making her crave large, strong, and callused.

"Sasha, and I'm just the sex-toy marketeer."

His eyes darkened deliciously at that. "I doubt you're *just* anything."

"Perry's my brother," Valerie said. "He used to be in our book club before he moved to Topeka, like a dweeb."

His hand began to slip from Sasha's, and she jerked her palm from his. They'd held on too long. "You were in *this* book club?" she asked. He was one of the Raunchies?

"Yes. I like to read," he said, as if it were that simple.

Which, really, *it was.*

"That's awesome," she said. *And sexy.* She kept that part to herself.

"Hey Perry, have you read the newest Minnesota Motorcycle Club book?" asked Andie, a petite black woman. She was wearing an ugly Christmas sweater with kittens on the front and had slapped a nametag on her chest that said, *Holiday Pussy.* Sasha wanted to be her best friend.

Perry smiled warmly. "I haven't. I DNF'ed the last one, but maybe I'll give the new a shot," he said.

Most of that went over Sasha's head, so she returned

to her seat and sat primly, waiting for the group to calm down again. After the excitement of Perry's arrival wore off, Sasha looked to Valerie to see if she could continue.

"Right! Sorry, Sasha. We'll let you wrap up, then we'll dive into our game of Dirty Book Dirty Santa."

"Sounds good." Sasha eyed Perry, who'd pulled a folding chair into the circle and was watching her, unconcerned.

It wouldn't be the first time she'd hand-sold sex toys to men, but he made her skin prickle. Made her feel squirmy and excited all at once.

She cleared her throat. "As I was saying, here are our prostate massagers. Use lube."

She directed that last comment at Perry. Rosiness rushed up his cheeks above the line of his beard as he smiled. A blusher. Mayday, too cute for words!

Without stopping to swoon, she continued, "I've also got a catalog for lingerie and underthings that you're welcome to peruse. Our lingerie is size and gender inclusive with a select range of bras, garters, slips, undies, binders, compression gaffs, and strap-on bottoms, all with Lady Robin's rock-and-roll flair. Now, does anyone have any questions?"

Louise raised her hand timidly.

"Yes?"

Louise bit her lip and glanced at Perry. He was a former Raunchy, so they were probably used to him being present, but Louise was obviously not comfortable asking this question in front of him.

Perry stood up abruptly. "Oh man, that eggnog smells

amazing. I'll be back." He rushed toward the breakfast room where the food and drinks were set up. With a smile, Sasha watched his long legs and tight ass waltz from the room.

He was a blusher *and* considerate of women's feelings. She wanted a bite.

Once he was gone, Louise laughed. "Gosh, sorry. I couldn't ask this in front of him. Do you have anything in double-F sizing?"

"Definitely. Everything, including our bralettes."

A few other book club members had questions about sizing and prices as well. As Sasha answered, another huge gust of wind made the house shudder and the lights flicker. She needed to hurry so she could get home before the roads were too treacherous for her Bug.

"Here are the order forms. I have some stock with me today, but if I don't have what you want, we guarantee its arrival in five business days anywhere in the continental US. Feel free to check out the items on display. If no one has any questions, I'm going to run to the restroom real quick."

Valerie directed Sasha to the closest bathroom in a hallway off the huge, gorgeous kitchen, which was also decorated with all manner of garland and Christmas candles. There was a centerpiece made of a grapevine wreath, red garden roses, and berries on the kitchen island. Sasha stopped and stared at it, her heartbeat in her throat.

It was eerily similar to the centerpieces she'd made a year ago for her wedding, only a lot fancier. Like a gut punch, it halted her in her tracks. Blood suddenly thundered in her ears, and her stomach pitched, a metallic taste hitting the back of her tongue. She had to squelch the urge to swipe the centerpiece off the counter and hurried out of the room instead.

Once Sasha was alone in the hallway, she leaned against the wall and tried to slow the frantic patter of her heartbeat. Her phone buzzed in her hand, which was more effective in distracting her than the deep breathing.

It was a weather alert. They were in a Blizzard Warning.

*Fucking great.*

She also had a text message from her older sister, Rosie.

Rosie: *Roads are horrible on the west side of city. Hope you're not out being wild.*

Sasha: *I'm wrapping up a Lady Robin's party. Will leave soon.*

Rosie was a worrier and a pessimist. Sasha was sure their little brother, Benji, had received a similar message.

Rosie: *Who the hell plans a sex toy party right before X-mas? You need to get home now!*

A laugh worked its way out of Sasha's throat, surprising her.

Sasha: *The dirtiest and coolest book club ever, that's who. Sex toys make the best stocking stuffers.*

Rosie: *Very funny.*

Sasha: *I am. I'll text when I leave. This place is out in the boonies, so I have at least an hour drive to get home.*

It wasn't really the boonies. There were plenty of

other properties around, but to a city girl like Sasha, it might as well have been the great frontier.

"Sasha?"

She jumped at Perry's deep voice and bobbled her phone until it slithered through her fingers and skittered across the floor. Thank God for super-protective cases.

"*Baby Jesus!* Stop making me drop things."

"Sorry. I didn't mean to startle you."

He swooped down and picked up her cell phone. Their fingers brushed when he handed it back, and she shivered. He smelled of cedar.

She liked it. A lot.

Maybe he was a lumberjack. He *was* wearing flannel.

He smiled, his eyes bright. "I feel like I crashed your sales pitch. I'm sorry if I made it awkward."

"Don't worry. I'm not shy."

His gaze landed on her lips before jerking away. "I think half the book club is heading out soon, and the rest are staying at the inn to wait out the storm. They're drawing names for a book exchange rather than playing Dirty Santa."

"Oh, that's good. I'll go get their orders, so I can head home too."

He took a deep breath. "This might be out of line but would you go to dinner with me sometime this week?"

Her pulse galloped off like a herd of reindeer. She hadn't been on a *date* date in ages. Dates led to expectations and crossed boundaries. She hadn't dated since … well, since the worst Christmas ever had soured the idea of relationships for her forever. Being left at the altar on Christmas Eve did that to you.

Rather than spill her issues on an unsuspecting hot guy, she said, "A date? All you know about me is that I sell sex toys for a living."

Some people thought that made her available or even a slut.

"No. I know you're smart and confident, and I like your voice. There's this lilt when you speak, like you're always having a great time and everything is funny. And your hair. I like your hair."

"Wow. Thank you."

A few of her regular lovers had not been fans of her hair when she'd chopped it into a pixie cut a few months ago. Needless to say, they weren't her lovers anymore.

He ran an unsteady hand across his chin and lips. In the darkness of the hallway, she couldn't see his eyes clearly. She wondered what color they were, wanted to see them alight with pleasure. She had a feeling Perry would be delightfully expressive and genuine in bed.

"I'm not the best at this," he said, voice shaky.

"You're actually doing pretty awesome."

"Really?"

"Yeah, really, but I'm not the dating type. And regardless, don't you live in Topeka?"

His smile withered, and she had the irrational urge to cup his cheek.

What was happening to her?

She wanted to blame her sudden soppy, sweet feelings on the Christmas cheer in the air. It was like those parasitic spores that latched onto everything, multiplied, then smothered their host.

"I *did* live in Topeka. I, uh, I'm not … My living situation is complicated."

"I'm not in the market for complicated," she said. "Though, you're super cute, so I'd probably be game for a night together. A one-night stand, basically. But not tonight because, you know, snow and ice and rear-wheel drive. I need to get home."

His mouth had gone a little slack, and she inwardly cringed. She tended to steamroll people. Men especially expected her to be more circumspect about her sexual appetites and romantic boundaries, but that wasn't her problem. It was theirs.

"I'm sorry. I can't tell if you're rejecting me or propositioning me," he finally said. The corners of his eyes crinkled.

"Both."

"I like you," he said decisively, and she laughed.

"I'm a bit much, I've been told. I like to fuck, eat, masturbate, and read, and I don't do any of those in moderation. Still interested?"

She had no idea why she was unleashing all her sass on him. Maybe to scare him off. Or to see if he'd stick around.

"I'm definitely still interested, Sasha."

"Then here's my number." She rattled it off for him, and he hurriedly input it into his cell.

They smiled at each other like two dorky teenagers before the sound of someone humming a Christmas carol in the kitchen jolted them apart.

"I'll be out in a second to wrap up everyone's orders. I need to hit the road before the Bug can't make it up the driveway," she said.

"I wondered whose car that was."

"My baby brother restored it for me a couple years ago. He's a little genius." She grinned just thinking about her brother, who at six foot four was in no way little or a baby.

"It's beautiful."

"I know." She winked and slipped into the bathroom.

The partiers were almost done drawing names for their romance novel exchange when she returned, so Sasha prepared to fill and file their orders.

Once they wrapped up, she clapped her hands once. "Okay, Staunchly Raunchy Book Club, does anyone have questions? I'm ready to take your orders if you have any."

A stack of order forms were passed in her direction. Her payout for this party would be a nice holiday bonus. Maybe she'd take her siblings out to their favorite Chinese restaurant on Christmas Day.

It took her about ten minutes to distribute the stock she had with her, accept payments, fill out receipts, and file the remaining orders. By the time she'd sold her last Love Bite, the wind was howling and whipping snow against the huge windows of the hearth room.

She didn't even have an ice scraper in her car. Her grandmother was probably rolling in her grave over how unprepared Sasha was for bad weather.

"Thank you for doing this," Valerie said with a solemnity that might have been due to too much mulled wine.

Louise nodded and bit her lip. "I've wanted to try out a vibrator, but I've been too self-conscious to go into a shop, and I wasn't sure how to pick one online. Some of the companies look sketchy."

"That's why I love this job. We want to make it easier and more comfortable for people to find and purchase what they want and need," Sasha said, dropping her voice to give the three of them privacy. "Sex toys are fun, and they're essential for some people, particularly women, to get off. There's nothing shameful or wrong about that. Technology is a wonderful thing."

"*Exactly*," Louise whispered, tucking her long, frizzy brown hair behind her ears. "We read so many sex-positive romance novels where the heroines have all this sexual agency, but here I am—too chickenshit to buy a vibrator. Well, no more. I bought two."

"Good." Sasha grinned at her and made a mental note to include a couple of coupons with Louise and Valerie's orders. "I'm happy you scheduled Lady Robin's for your holiday party. This was such a fun group."

"You're welcome to join the book club! We're always excited to indoctrinate unsuspecting humans into our romance novel cult," Valerie pitched in.

"Thank you, but I'm not exactly local. I live on the far side of the city, over an hour away, but I'd love book recommendations. I enjoy thrillers, so maybe romantic suspense? I'll give you my email."

Valerie whooped and rushed off to get a pen and

paper. Sasha smiled in her wake. Valerie was beautiful, especially now, when she was flushed, uninhibited, and excited about books. Perry and Valerie both had dark curly hair and killer smiles. They could have been twins. But there was something about Perry, something that hit her right in the chest.

What was that exactly? Chemistry, maybe? Lust? Sometimes she was knocked over by it, by that rush of adrenaline and discomfort, when she wanted someone. When the thrumming in her pulse spiked from, *Oh, I like their smile,* to, *Oh, I want to sit on their face.* But this dose of Perry felt exceptionally potent.

Gender had never factored into it for her. She liked women. She liked men. And she liked people who were both or neither or fluid. But regardless of gender, she had a type.

*Unexpected. Adventurous. Expressive. Emotional.*

She had no idea if Perry had any or all those characteristics, but she couldn't help but hope he'd call her eventually so she could find out.

Valerie rushed back over with a notepad and pen as Sasha finished packing up her bag of unsold toys. Sasha was writing out her email address for Valerie when Perry materialized beside them.

Sasha, of course, jumped at his sudden appearance and dropped the fucking pen. He picked it up for her.

"Dray is giving a bunch of people a ride home since they have that huge minivan with the all-wheel drive. Andie and Karen are hoping to stay here until the storm clears if you have space," Perry told Valerie.

"We have enough rooms," Valerie said.

"Do you have space for me too?" Louise asked.

"Absolutely." Valerie winked at Louise, which made her blush. Then Valerie turned to Sasha. "Will you be able to make it home? You could stay here. We always have room at this inn."

"Oh, uh. No, I better not." Sasha glanced at Perry. It was tempting, but she didn't think she could survive the Christmas extravaganza going on at this place for longer than a few more minutes. "I appreciate the offer, though."

"Of course," Valerie said. "Thanks again for coming. I think I've officially hosted the best Staunchly Raunchy Book Club Christmas Party ever."

"Yeah, those toys will make awesome stocking stuffers," Perry said.

"That's what I said!" Sasha exclaimed. "Batteries not included, though." Perry tipped his head back and laughed, his whole face transforming, opening up with humor and happiness. And oh man, she loved a good laugh. She had to wrench her gaze away from him before she was caught staring. "I'm going to brave the weather and head out."

Valerie, amazingly, gave her a hug before she hurried away to see the other guests off. An unusual emotion lumped in Sasha's throat at the two seconds of friendly contact. She wasn't much of a hugger. Her grandma had been the bearer of hugs in the family, and maybe she and her siblings had been working at a deficit, because a platonic hug from a stranger at Christmas shouldn't have made her want to bawl.

Perry's voice brought her out of her navel gazing. "It's bad out there. You sure you'll be okay?" He was watching her closely. Now she could see that he had hazel eyes, an intriguing mix of green and brown. The lights from the Christmas tree reflected in them like stars.

"I'll be fine."

"All right. I'll walk you out."

She donned her coat and trudged out into the snow, pulling her two roller bags of sex toys—lighter than when she'd first arrived—behind her.

The snow was mixed with pelting ice. The door handle on her VW Bug was so cold it burned her hand when she opened it. Perry helped her load the bags.

A solid coating of ice covered the back window, but it wasn't as thick on the sides and front. She turned the car on and flipped the heater to defrost.

"I don't have an ice scraper," she said, embarrassed. She was a strong, capable, independent woman, and it sucked to be caught unprepared. She parked in a parking garage at her apartment and at work, so her car wasn't sitting out in the elements very often.

"I think I have two. Hold on." He rushed over to a hulking silver SUV and pulled one long-handled and one smaller scraper out of the backseat. He handed her the bigger one, then without a word, started in on the back window.

She attacked the ice on the front window with a vengeance, taking out her frustration, sexual and other-wise. She was seriously regretting the red velvet dress, thigh-high fishnets, and black stilettos. This was the worst winter-weather outfit ever, and her coat wasn't doing much to cut the cold.

They finished quickly, which was great, since Sasha was freezing her snowballs off.

Perry took a step closer to her. He had snow frosting his dark curls and beard.

"I don't feel good about this. The weather is atrocious," he said.

"I'll be fine," she repeated, glancing up the huge hill she'd have to drive to make it out of the Winterberry Inn's driveway. It was an ice rink. If ice rinks had a twelve percent grade. This was a horrible idea.

"I'm going to text you, so you have my number. Will you call if you have any issues getting home?" Perry asked.

"Sure. It was nice to meet you, Perry. I hope you text me sometime but, you know, not just because of a little winter weather."

"Oh, I plan to." He swooped in and kissed her briefly on the cheek, barely a touch. But his lips were warm against her chilled skin, and it sent a shimmery arc of heat through her. She shivered, and he must have misinterpreted it, because he opened her driver's side door, and said, "Get in before you catch a chill."

*Catch a chill?* She was mouthing those words to herself, a small smile flirting on the edges of her mouth, as she put the car into gear. What an old-fashioned phrase. Perry waved at her, and her smile grew. She started the steep climb up the driveway.

Maybe Perry was really into those historical romances

her sister enjoyed—the ones with dukes and scandals and carriage rides. She could almost see him as a brooding Regency hero, except his smile was too unrestrained.

Next she imagined him shirtless and in a clench with a woman in a beautiful fancy dress, because why not? It was such a pleasant fantasy that the first skid of her baby's tires came as a total surprise.

Adrenaline exploded in her gut like a pipe bomb.

She was suddenly too hot, and the sticky, bitter taste of fear burst on her tongue.

What if her car's traction wasn't good enough to get up the hill? Her engine was a dinosaur. She was a month late on changing the oil because she was obviously irresponsible.

Then her Bug shuddered, the tires stopped spinning, and the car slipped backward.

## Also by Erin McLellan

### Farm College Series

*Controlled Burn*

*Clean Break*

### Love Life Series

*Life on Pause*

*Life of Bliss*

### Storm Chasers Series

*Natural Disaster*

### So Over the Holidays Series

*Stocking Stuffers*

*Candy Hearts*

## Acknowledgments

A huge thank you to everyone who has read and loved the So Over the Holidays series. The Holiday siblings were a joy to write, and I couldn't have done it without your support.

An extra big thanks to Edie Danford for her amazing editing, Susie Selva for being a rockstar proofreader, Cate Ashwood for the dream-worthy cover, Judith at A Novel Take PR for the great promo, Karen for the beta notes, and Allison for the (dreaded) blurb help. Also a huge shout out to the authors who inspired me and kept me writing this book when it got hard (Allison, Layla, Lisa, M.A., Karen, Annabeth, and so many more).

Hugs and kisses to my family.

## About the Author

Erin McLellan is the author of the Farm College, So Over the Holidays, and Storm Chasers series. She enjoys writing happily ever afters that are earthy, emotional, quirky, humorous, and very sexy. Originally from Oklahoma, she currently lives in Alaska and spends her time dreaming up queer contemporary romances. She is a lover of chocolate, college sports, antiquing, Dr Pepper, and binge-worthy TV shows.

CPSIA information can be obtained
at www.ICGtesting.com
Printed in the USA
LVHW092125040621
689427LV00001B/2